DEADLY HERITAGE

A
GEORGIA RAE WINSTON
MYSTERY

MARISSA SHROCK

CIMELIAPRESS

Deadly Heritage

© 2019 by Marissa Shrock

Cover art ©Jennifer Zemanek/Seedlings Design Studio

Scriptures taken from the Holy Bible, New International Version®, NIV®. Copyright © 1973, 1978, 1984, 2011 by Biblica, Inc.™ Used by permission of Zondervan. All rights reserved worldwide. www.zondervan.com The "NIV" and "New International Version" are trademarks registered in the United States Patent and Trademark Office by Biblica, Inc.™

Published by Cimelia Press, Greentown, Indiana

Printed in the United States of America

Print ISBN-13: 978-0-9969879-4-3

Library of Congress Control Number: 2018914875

Whatever is has already been, and what will be has been before, and God will call the past to account.

Ecclesiastes 3:15

AUTHOR'S NOTE

Creating a story world is one of the best parts of being an author, and Richard County, Wildcat Springs, and Richardville are all fictional places, though I did use Central Indiana history and geography to guide my name choices. I also utilized some fictional license with police procedures to remain true to the pace of the story.

CHAPTER ONE

"Georgia, I insist."

Wanda Morris shoved a wedding gown at me, leaving me no choice but to grab it. That is, unless I wanted to let the pricey creation pool on the dressing room floor and risk the ire of the pixie-faced bridal consultant who was staring at me.

"We're here for *you*." I draped the beaded, halter gown over my arm. It really *was* pretty—and a cut that would look good on my tall, curvy frame. I never should've stopped to admire it, because today wasn't about me.

Wanda was going to marry Grandpa Winston in a little over a week, and she'd gathered a small entourage of friends and family who were available on a Thursday afternoon for her final fitting at Mary Ann's Bridal Boutique in downtown Richardville, Indiana.

"You'll need a dress soon enough, so you should start getting ideas." Her brown eyes gleamed with mischief.

"But Cal and I haven't—"

"Talked about marriage?" Wanda put her hands on her hips. "Why on earth not?"

1

While I hoped our relationship was headed there, we hadn't discussed getting hitched, even though we'd been dating since last fall. I certainly hadn't expected an engagement ring for Valentine's Day, which we'd celebrated last night by having Wednesday Night Wings at Pizza Heaven in our hometown of Wildcat Springs.

Not the most romantic of dates, but we didn't want to fight the crowds, and Cal was preoccupied thanks to a new case. Besides, he was planning to take me to my favorite Italian restaurant for my birthday tonight.

"We're not in a hurry." I ignored the uncertainty rippling through my gut and shot a helpless look at Wanda's friend Beverly Alspaugh, who was Cal's great-aunt and my neighbor.

"Wanda, how about we let Georgia and Cal figure out their relationship." Beverly stood and took the bridal burden off my arm. "They're young, and there's no need to rush into anything." With her back to Wanda, she winked at me.

"I don't know." Wanda brushed aside her silver side bangs, part of an asymmetrical haircut that took ten years off her appearance. "By the time I was thirty-one, I'd been married ten years."

Nothing like a reminder on my birthday about how I've failed at landing a mate. I wound a strand of my long, honey-blond hair around my finger.

"Things are different now." Beverly handed the gown to the consultant who clicked away in her ridiculously high heels.

Mallory Morris, Wanda's daughter-in-law, looked up from her phone. "It's smart not to rush. Even though Tyler and I were high school sweethearts, we waited until after college to get married."

I'd been done with college for years, but I appreciated Mallory's diplomatic effort.

Beverly, Mallory, and I all gazed at Wanda.

"All right then." Wanda raised her hands in surrender. "Ron's said I've turned into a bridezilla, but I want everyone to be as happy as we are. I apologize for putting you on the spot."

"It's okay." I leaned over and gave her a hug. "I'll be sure to invite you when it's time for me to go dress shopping."

"Thanks, sweetie." Wanda clasped her hands as the seamstress entered with a garment bag that contained her dress. "Oh, I'm so excited! I never could've had anything like this when I was married the first time. Our wedding was in my parents' front room, and my mama cooked a pot roast."

She was fond of reminding us about these facts, which were the main reasons—to my grandpa's dismay—that she'd insisted on having a bigger wedding than he'd anticipated.

The seamstress hung the garment bag in a dressing room. "Let's see how it fits."

Wanda swished the curtain closed.

Beverly's flip phone rang, and she stepped over next to a sale rack to answer. Her kids hadn't been able to convince her to get a smart phone. At eighty, she'd lived most of her life without cellphones and didn't see the need for a fancy one now.

I plopped onto the pink, velvety couch next to Mallory. I fought the urge to call her Mrs. Morris because she'd been my high school government teacher. Her dad, Old Man Smith, was my other neighbor. In her mid-fifties and attractive, she was now the principal at Wildcat Springs Junior-Senior High and had taken the afternoon off to join us.

"How's your school year going?" I asked.

"Not bad, but we're all counting the days until spring break." She tucked her phone in her crocodile embossed purse. "I'm glad you're here today, because I've been meaning to call you."

"Really?" What on earth could she want from me?

"Would you be interested in filling in for my choir teacher, Mrs. Peterson, when she goes on maternity leave after spring break?" Mallory crossed her slender legs.

I had a degree in music education but had chosen to farm corn and soybeans with my grandpa after my daddy died. "Actually, that time would conflict with planting season, so I can't."

I thanked the Lord above for my good excuse.

"Oh, silly me. I should've thought of that." She fidgeted with her silver bangle bracelets. They complemented her black and white sheath dress, which showed a tad more cleavage than I would've been comfortable displaying in a school full of teenage boys.

"Thanks for thinking of me."

She flipped her wavy brown hair over her shoulder. "We'll get you in the classroom sometime. You'd be great."

Ummm. No. The thought of teaching junior high and high school was enough to make me want to pass out.

Beverly returned to the dressing room, and all the color had drained from her cheeks.

My eyes widened. Her cancer had been in remission for several months, and she still wore the curly gray wig that she'd purchased after starting chemo. Had her doctor called to tell her the cancer had returned? "Are you okay?"

She pressed her bright red lips together, glanced at Mallory, and then motioned toward Wanda, who was emerging from the dressing room.

Her silver, floor-length gown shimmered, and the three-quarter-length sleeves displayed intricate beadwork. She stepped onto the carpeted platform and twirled underneath the chandelier.

"It's beautiful," I said. "The silver looks stunning with your hair."

Beverly sank into a wingback chair. "Lovely."

"Ron will think you look hot," Mallory said.

Wanda lifted the skirt. "We should probably take up the hem a bit more."

The seamstress knelt and began putting in some pins. I gazed at Beverly, who was folding and unfolding her arthritis-bent hands. She shook her head, as if she knew I was about to ask what was wrong.

I nodded, but I'd find out soon enough. After all, there was a good reason for my reputation as an amateur sleuth.

***

When we finished at the bridal shop, I bolted to the parking lot and hopped in my truck. As I put on my seatbelt, my phone honked with the warning-alert ring tone I'd assigned to each of my twin stepbrothers.

This time it was Austin wanting to video chat. I'd better answer, or he'd keep calling until I did. "Hey, Austin."

Out of the corner of my eye, I noticed Beverly, Wanda, and Mallory walking toward Beverly's car that was parked next to the music store. What were they doing? They hadn't all come together.

"Hey, sissy. It's your favorite stepbrother." Austin grinned.

"Dude, I'm her favorite stepbro." Preston, Austin's identical twin, hovered over his shoulder. "She totally likes me better than you." He elbowed his brother.

Preston was slightly less annoying than Austin—though we'd all come a long way since my mom had married their dad five and a half years ago. "I love you idiots both equally." And it was my lucky day to get a two-for-one call.

"Sissy, I'm touched." Austin pressed his hand to his heart.

In the head.

I glanced outside as Beverly removed two manila envelopes from her car and handed one to Mallory and one to Wanda. What was she giving them?

"Earth to Georgia," Austin said.

"Sorry. I yanked my attention back to my stepbrothers.

"We're going to sing you a birthday rap." Preston put up the hood on his sweatshirt.

Austin donned a baseball cap.

Merciful heavens. "Go for it."

"Yo, yo, it's our girl Georgia's b-day, and we gotta let her know. She's the very best detective in the whole wide world. With us by her side, criminals can't hide. So happy. Birthday. To you." They both pointed at me.

I applauded. "Bravo!" My boyfriend might take issue with the best detective thing since he was a professional who worked for the Richard County Sheriff's Department, and I only dabbled in crime solving. "I like the part about criminals not being able to hide."

"When can we be your sidekicks again?" Even though the twins were twenty-four years old and semi-successful real estate agents, Austin could still whine like a seven-year-old boy.

I started my truck and cranked up the heat. "Probably not for a long time."

Although I'd learned to never say never when it came to solving mysteries. They seemed to find their way to me.

"Will you promise to let us know if you need us?" Austin hadn't lost the whine.

"Please?" Preston said.

"Yes. I have to go home and get ready for my date tonight, so I'll catch you guys later, okay?"

"Say hi to Cal for us." Austin winked.

Then they made kissing noises—in unison.

I stopped at the gas station in my one-stoplight hometown of Wildcat Springs and was filling my truck when I got a text from Beverly asking me to stop by. With a churning stomach, I made my way to her house—about half a mile down the road from mine.

Acres of empty brown fields—including some of my own—surrounded her property, which held a two-story white house with black shutters, an old-fashioned, paint-chipped barn, and a stable where her daughters had once kept horses. I parked my truck in the gravel driveway and hurried to the porch. A wooden snowman stood next to the door with his stick arms open in a friendly welcome. I shivered. Spring needed to get here fast because I was over the snow and cold.

Beverly opened the door before I could ring the bell. "Come on in."

A wave of vanilla candle hit my nose as I entered the house. Her black schnauzer, Miss Peacock, charged toward me with a yippy bark and pawed and sniffed my boots.

"Is it your cancer?" I blurted.

"No, no." Beverly closed the door and picked up her dog. "My health's fine." She stroked the dog's head. "I could tell that's what you were worried about."

I blew out a breath. "I'm so glad. I thought your doctor had called."

She nodded. "I figured as much. Lately, I've been feeling better than I have for months, thank the Lord. I've even felt well enough to start volunteering at the museum again."

Beverly had retired from teaching U.S. history at Wildcat Springs High School before I was old enough for her class. Now she channeled her love of the subject into volunteering at the history museum. It memorialized the town's past and drew in a decent number of tourists each year.

"I'm sure Wanda and the other volunteers are glad for the extra help."

"Yes." Beverly smiled, but a hint of concern lingered in her eyes.

I tucked my hair behind my ear. "Thanks for defending me today. I hate it when people badger me about getting married."

She waved a hand. "No problem. I'd love to see you and Cal end up together, but that's for God, Cal, and you to determine. You don't need pressure from other people to hurry down the aisle—even if they mean well."

I studied my boots. Had God shown me if my relationship with Cal was the right choice? Did I even want Him to, or did I want to make up my own mind?

"Anyway, I asked you to stop by so I could give you these old pictures." She reached over to her oak console table and picked up a thick manila envelope with my name on it. Another envelope, labeled *Earl Smith*, remained on the table. "I had them with me earlier, but I decided we needed to chat in private."

So that's what she'd given Wanda and Mallory.

"I've been cleaning out my closets and ran across a bunch of old pictures I thought my family and friends would like. There are several of you and your daddy." She handed me the envelope.

I lifted the flap and slid the pictures out. On top of the stack was a photo of Daddy and me in the combine cab. I was about three or so. Mom had styled my hair in pigtails, and I clutched a juice box and a bag of animal crackers. Beverly had probably flagged down my dad while he'd been harvesting our field behind her house and given us a snack. She'd done that a lot through the years. She was also a faithful prayer warrior, regularly asking God for justice after my daddy had been murdered and his case remained unsolved.

Tears pricked my eyes, and I slid the prints back into the envelope. "Thanks. I appreciate it." I tucked the package into my leopard-print shoulder bag.

"You're welcome."

She bent to release Miss Peacock and then straightened. "I haven't told many people this, but I've been emptying my guest room closet because Clara's coming home to stay with me for a while." There was no mistaking the apprehension in her tone—and expression.

"That's great!" I'd never met Beverly's daughter, because she'd left town long before I was born and hadn't even made an appearance for her father's funeral five years earlier.

"Yes." Beverly smoothed her floral blouse's hem. "She hasn't set foot in Wildcat Springs for thirty-eight years. Bill and I went to visit her a few times in Texas, and she's always been good to call once a month, but she hasn't had much to do with us." Beverly's eyes watered.

"I'm so sorry."

She nodded and swiped under her eyes. "I'm thankful the Lord is leading her home. I've been praying for years that she'd come back and face whatever drove her away."

"Are you worried about the visit?"

"Truthfully, yes. Denise called to vent when we were at the bridal shop because she's never gotten over how her little sister abandoned the family." Beverly shook her head. "Plus, she and Jack have separated, so this added stress is throwing her for a loop. I didn't want to mention my family's business in front of Mallory since she loves gossip—just like her dad." Beverly pressed her lips together.

Old Man Smith definitely loved gossip. Not to mention, Wanda wasn't the most discreet woman in the world. "When's Clara getting here?"

Beverly glanced at the grandfather clock nestled in the corner of her formal living room. "A few hours. I hope she makes it in before all the snow we're supposed to get."

I furrowed my brow. "How much?" I usually kept better track of the weather, because I had a plow that I'd put on my truck to clear out driveways for my friends.

"We're in the eight-to-ten-inches band—the storm shifted farther south than the meteorologists thought it would last night."

Yikes. I'd be busy tomorrow morning. "I'd better scoot. Cal and I are going out for my birthday." I hugged her. "Thanks again for the pictures." I opened the door.

"You're welcome, dearie." She smiled.

"See you later." I waved as I jogged to my truck.

Cal walked in the back door of my farmhouse while whistling "Brown-Eyed Girl." He held two plastic grocery sacks. "Change of plans. I'm cooking for you tonight since we're supposed to get snow." Concern filled his blue eyes. "I hope you're not disappointed."

"Nope. I'm thrilled when you cook." I gazed up at my handsome boyfriend. I towered over a lot of men, so I loved that Cal had a few inches on me.

He set the groceries on the bench in my foyer while he took off his black leather jacket. Gus, my yellow Labrador retriever puppy, nosed the sacks, and I snatched them away before he could do any damage.

He'd developed a new quirk—digging in trashcans. Not even an entire container of cayenne pepper sprinkled all over the garbage had deterred that crazy animal. All of my bathroom trashcans now sat on the backs of the toilets, and my new kitchen wastebasket had a secure lid.

"Hey," Cal said in his sexy, resonant voice. "Come here, birthday girl." He drew me into an embrace and gave me a gentle kiss on the lips.

There'd better be more of that later. "What're we having?" I smoothed his dark, windblown hair.

He dimpled, and my heart skipped a beat. "Chicken and

roasted vegetables." He brushed some hair out of my eyes. "I'll take you to Salvador's another time for your birthday dinner."

"It's fine. As long as we're together." Then I chuckled.

"What's so funny?"

"Six months ago, I would've rather been gagged than say something so sappy."

Sometimes it felt too good to be true that I'd met someone like Cal and that he liked me back. We headed into the kitchen, where I set the grocery sacks on the table.

"Wow. I had no idea you were so cynical." He arched an eyebrow. "I just can't imagine that."

"Shut up." I pretended to launch a sweet potato at him.

He emptied the sacks and put the groceries on the counter in my 1980s kitchen—which was begging for an update that I hadn't gotten around to. Maybe I was secretly fond of the linoleum flooring and pastel flower-basket print wallpaper in this house where I'd grown up.

Nah.

He stopped and looked around the kitchen. "Please tell me you have a cookie sheet." He pointed to the groceries. "Because I'm making a sheet pan meal, and if you don't . . ."

I opened the cabinet next to my oven. "No worries." I removed a set of three cookie sheets wrapped in plastic and displayed them like a spokesmodel. "Ta-da."

"How long have those been in there like that?" He found a knife in the drawer next to my sink and began rinsing and peeling sweet potatoes.

I poked my finger through the plastic and ripped it off. "Since, this summer?" I squinted and pursed my lips. "Mom got them for me on sale, but as long as Brandi keeps me supplied with cookies, I don't need to bake my own."

Unless he wanted a cookie-baking girlfriend and was disappointed that I never brought him homemade treats. But he didn't have a big sweet tooth, so it shouldn't matter, right?

He chuckled. "Great excuse."

Time to steer the conversation away from my inadequacies. "You'll find this interesting. Beverly told me Clara's coming home for a visit tonight." I set the largest cookie sheet on the counter and put the other two back in the cabinet.

He stopped peeling. "Really. She say why?"

"No." I leaned against the island. "Why hasn't she been home all this time? Beverly's never talked about it."

"I have no idea." Cal set a naked sweet potato aside and picked up a second one. "It's always been a hush-hush topic in the family. My impression's always been that Clara never quite fit in here."

Interesting. It wasn't my business anyway. "How was work today?"

"Fine."

"Have you been able to identify the body yet?"

On Monday afternoon, a construction worker had unearthed skeletal remains in the woods while digging a foundation for a new house in the western part of the county.

"Not yet. I hope we can give a family some closure soon." He put down a sweet potato. "Did I tell you Marvin's replacement started on Monday?"

Marvin Kimball was the detective who'd worked with Cal—until he'd gotten himself in trouble with the law. "No. Nothing like jumping right in with a big case. Are you getting along?"

"Yep. She's nice. Name's Vanessa Hawk. Grew up in Richardville, and she's around your age. You know her?" He began chopping the peeled sweet potatoes into chunks.

Gus's claws clicked over the floor, and he stopped next to Cal.

"No. I don't know everybody in Richard County." *She.* I

swallowed. *Don't be stupid, Georgia.* Is that why he hadn't remembered to tell me? "What's she like?"

Here, fishy-fishy.

I walked to the sink, squirted some dish soap on the cookie sheet, and scrubbed it.

"She's tough. Great instincts. Been with the department for about seven years." He cut the second potato. "She'll be good to work with."

"Is she married?" I kept my voice nice and casual.

"Engaged."

I squeezed the dishcloth and hated myself for the "Hallelujah Chorus" playing in my head. I sneaked a look at him out of the corner of my eye. He hadn't stopped chopping and seemed oblivious to the fact that I was having a moment. Good. The last thing I wanted was for Cal to think I was insecure about our relationship.

As I rinsed and dried the cookie sheet, I thought of my late grandma Winston's penchant for spouting off maxims and assigning them random numbers. After her death, her habit lived on in my head, and one of the most important principles throbbed in my mind.

Life Lesson #15: Insecurity ruins relationships.

"What else can I do to help?" I took in the red onion and the package of chicken sitting on the counter.

He winked. "Relax and keep me company." He wiped his hands on his jeans and looked around the kitchen. "I'll be right back. I forgot to bring in your cake."

"Is it chocolate?"

"Sure is."

"Perfect." I tossed the dishtowel on the counter. "I'll run out and get it. You keep cooking."

I needed a gulp of fresh air.

Later that night, it still hadn't started snowing, which didn't break my heart because that meant Cal could stick around and watch *Murder on the Orient Express*. His dinner had been fabulous, and he'd purchased a cake in the shape of a gold clutch purse from Pastry Delight in Wildcat Springs.

I'd snapped pictures of the cake, along with the red roses he'd gotten me yesterday for Valentine's Day, to show my best friends Brandi and Ashley, but I wasn't one of those women who felt the need to brag to everyone on social media. Although, I'd have plenty to say because of how good Cal was to me. I couldn't ask for a better boyfriend.

He'd even gotten me a silver necklace with a key-shaped pendant, which I'd put on immediately.

We finished the movie and watched the eleven o'clock news to get an explanation as to why the snow hadn't materialized. The meteorologist was in the middle of promising an inch of snowfall per hour when the wail of approaching sirens interrupted.

Cal and I exchanged glances.

"Those are close." I tossed a throw pillow aside and shot off the couch. With Gus at my heels, I bolted to the front door, threw it open, and stepped onto the porch. Cal followed.

A sheriff's deputy's car whizzed by. Down the road, blue and red lights flashed, and my heart dropped to my feet.

"They're at Beverly's," I whispered and grasped the porch railing.

Lord, please help her.

"Get your shoes and coat." Cal was already back inside, putting on his jacket and stepping into his shoes.

I slipped on the first pair of sneakers I could find, shut Gus in his crate, and tugged on my coat as I ran out the door. Cal was already waiting in his Jeep with the engine running.

We traveled the short distance to Beverly's house in silence, and when we arrived, two cars from the sheriff's department and an ambulance were parked next to the house, along with a red hatchback that I guessed was Clara's. A third car from the sheriff's department blocked the driveway.

My breath hitched. This was more than a health emergency.

Cal parked his Jeep on the side of the road and left it running. "Stay in here."

I nodded, because a lump the size of Alaska had taken up residence in my throat.

He jumped out and jogged over to the car at the end of the driveway as a few stray snowflakes swirled around him. A deputy emerged from the car and started talking and pointing at the house.

I opened the window, but the gusting wind drowned out their voices.

Cal's shoulders sagged, and he ran his fingers through his hair. Then he turned and trudged toward me. Halfway to the Jeep, he stopped and answered his phone.

"Perkins." He listened, pain filling his expression. "Already here. I'll be in shortly." He disconnected and shoved his phone in his jacket pocket.

My chest constricted.

No. No. No! I balled my fingers into a fist. *Please, God. Don't let it be . . .*

Cal opened the passenger-side door.

I swallowed. "What happened?" But deep down I already knew.

He scrubbed his hands over his face. "Aunt Beverly was murdered."

CHAPTER TWO

K ittens.

I didn't consider myself a cat person, and I was recently a converted dog person, but all I could see were the kittens Beverly had given my brother Dakota and me when we were growing up. My favorite had been an orange and white one I'd named Peaches, though we'd had black, gray, and calico cats as well.

"Georgia?" Cal leaned into the Jeep and grasped my hand. "Are you okay?"

"Beverly used to give Dakota and me kittens. In fact, the cats out in my barn are their descendants. She gave us so many that when we went trick-or-treating at her place, Mom always warned us we'd better come home with just candy because Beverly could always talk Daddy into taking a kitten or two. Dakota always tried to get Mom to let us have a house cat, and—"

"Georgia." Concern lingered in Cal's eyes as he rested his hands on my shoulders.

I reined my thoughts back, unbuckled my seatbelt, and slid out. "How?" I whispered.

"Gunshot wound to the chest." He wrapped his arms around me.

I closed my eyes and buried my face in his shoulder, and for a moment, he held me and stroked my hair while I inhaled the comforting scent of his cologne and leather jacket.

I lifted my head. "Why?" I could barely say the word.

"We don't know yet, but it looks like she interrupted a break-in."

I shuddered. That's what they'd said about my daddy—he'd interrupted a break-in.

The sheriff's department detectives theorized that when Daddy was on his way home from a school board meeting that night, he saw suspicious activity at the grain elevator. Because he was a good citizen, he stopped to investigate since there'd been vandalism there the week before. The robbers shot him and escaped. With no security cameras, the case was impossible to crack. Beverly's late husband Bill owned the elevator, but she'd sold it after he died of a heart attack.

"I'm sorry, but I need to go." He stepped back and squeezed my hand. "Take the Jeep. I'll pick it up at your house when we're done here."

I nodded. "Are *you* okay?" He'd have to deal with the blood and gore.

"Yeah. I'll call you later." He kissed my forehead and turned to go.

"Cal?"

"Yeah?" He faced me.

"Check to see if Miss Peacock's okay. Beverly loved that dog. I can . . . I'm willing to take her until I can find her a home. I don't want her to go to a shelter. She's old and might not get adopted."

He gave me a sad smile. "Will do." He strode toward the farmhouse as the slow-to-arrive snow finally made its entrance with a vengeance.

Taking a deep breath, I closed the Jeep's door, walked around the vehicle, got in the driver's seat, and gazed at the porch. My eyes fell on Beverly's cheerful snowman—so innocent and out of place. I leaned back against the headrest and didn't bother fighting the fresh wave of tears that blurred my vision and spilled over.

Why hadn't I taken more time with Beverly earlier? When she'd been battling cancer, I'd always been mindful that each conversation might be our last. I yanked my gloves out of my pockets and used them to dab my tears. Even though I only had to drive about half a mile, I didn't want to move until I pulled myself together.

Tap. Tap. Tap.

Beverly's and my neighbor, Earl "Old Man" Smith, tipped his Vietnam veteran's baseball cap and waved. "Hey there, Miss Georgia."

I opened the window. "Hey."

He pointed toward the house. "What's going on? I heard the sirens and walked down to check it out."

"Someone shot Beverly." I sniffed. "She's dead." The lump in my throat threatened to choke me.

His jaw dropped, and his large ears seemed to stick out even more. "You sure?" He grabbed a hold of the Jeep.

"Yes, sir. Cal confirmed it."

Earl removed his hat and pressed it against his chest. Seconds ticked by, and he swallowed hard, as if he were trying to hold himself together. "Beverly was a fine woman. She and my Becky used to can green beans together every summer."

Earl had been a widower for at least twenty years, and I barely remembered his wife.

He cleared his throat. "Stopped by and talked to her earlier this evening." He glanced at the baby-faced deputy guarding the driveway entrance. "Had some old pictures she needed to give me," he added quickly, even though the wind was drowning out our conversation. "Never dreamed tonight would be the last time I talked to her." He put his hat back on.

"Yes." My voice sounded faraway, and I looked at the deputy. He eyed us as he got back in his car, but seeing as how we weren't trying to breach the crime scene's perimeter, there wasn't any reason for him to shoo us away—yet.

My desire to find justice for Beverly began to break through the shock of losing her, and Earl was clearly a wealth of information. Besides, I needed something else to focus on, so I didn't start sobbing. "Hop in. I'll give you a ride home."

"I'd appreciate that. My arthritis is acting up." He ambled around the vehicle, brushed off the snow, and got in.

Pushing away my sorrow, I focused on getting Earl to spill details. "Did you notice anything strange tonight?" Town lore had him yoked to a pair of binoculars that he used on a regular basis—a rumor I was mindful of every time I stepped outside into my yard.

He scratched his chin. "About nine-thirty, I was letting my dog out when I heard a vehicle go by real slow-like, playing music so loud it scared old Boomer. I shooed him inside and walked around the house for a look-see. Little gray sedan with a couple of teenagers carrying on. They headed toward Beverly's house but passed on by, so I didn't think much of it."

I glanced toward Beverly's house as I put the Jeep in drive. "Did you get a look at the plate?"

"Nah. Don't see too well. You think they coulda been casing Beverly's place and come back later?"

"Possibly." I threw the Jeep into park. "You should report what you saw." I reached into my coat pocket to retrieve my phone, so I could text Cal, but in my hurry to get to Beverly's, I'd left it behind. I got out and walked over to the deputy guarding the scene. Earl trailed behind me.

"Evening, ma'am," he said. "I can't let you past this car, but is there something I can help with?"

I motioned toward Earl. "This gentleman and I are Beverly's neighbors, and we were talking about what happened. Mr. Smith might have information that Detective Perkins would be interested in knowing. I'd text him myself, but I left my phone at home, so could you call and ask him to come talk to us at his convenience?"

"I'll take care of it, Deputy Kerns," a woman said.

I faced her. Even though she wore a hooded parka, her pretty face and willowy frame made her look as though she'd be more at home in a magazine shoot than at a crime scene.

She extended her hand. "Detective Vanessa Hawk."

"Georgia Winston." I grasped her gloved hand and shook. My boyfriend had failed to mention his new partner was gorgeous. But why would he?

Thank goodness she was engaged.

She smiled, displaying perfect white teeth. "Cal's girlfriend. Nice to meet you." Then her expression grew serious as she turned to Earl. "Now what did you see, sir?"

I stepped back and flailed my arms as I nearly lost my footing on the slickening pavement.

Smooth, Georgia Rae.

I gazed at Beverly's house as Earl repeated what he'd told me. Cal was standing on the porch talking to a stocky woman with chin-length hair. She clutched Miss Peacock to her chest.

She had to be Clara. Had she found Beverly? She'd said her daughter would be there this evening, so the timing would be right. My heart ached for her.

Cal walked her to the deputy's car at the end of the driveway and opened the door. Still holding the dog, she slid into the back seat. Was she a suspect? Were they taking her in for questioning? Surely not with Miss Peacock in tow.

Cal strode toward us.

Detective Hawk met Cal at the end of the driveway. "I'm so sorry about your aunt."

"Me too." He made eye contact with me and then turned his focus back to Detective Hawk.

"What do we know so far?" she asked.

I moved a few steps closer and strained to hear Cal over the wind.

"Beverly's daughter Clara came for a visit tonight. They ate dinner, went to bed, and Clara woke up to the sound of a gunshot. She grabbed her gun and started down the stairs. When she rounded the landing, a masked intruder fired at her. Clara took cover and shot back. Grazed the shooter's coat sleeve. When the intruder fled, Clara found her mother dead on the kitchen floor. Called 911."

"A break-in?" Detective Hawk asked.

"Looks that way. Patio door's glass was shattered. Beverly's wallet is on the floor along with the rest of her purse's contents. Credit cards are there but no cash. Not sure what else is missing yet."

Detective Hawk squinted at the house. "Does Clara have a military or law enforcement background?"

"No. Self-defense instructor in Texas. Has a permit to carry a concealed weapon."

They tromped toward the house, and I turned to Earl. "We should go. There's nothing else for us to do."

We got back in the Jeep as a silver Chevy truck stopped behind us, and Beverly's son-in-law Jack Schultz hopped out.

I opened the window as he passed. "Jack!"

He turned back. "Georgia. What're you doing here?" In spite of the freezing temperatures, he wore only a Wildcat Football hoodie—he was head coach at the high school. His gray buzz cut made him look like he belonged in the army, and word on the street was that he ran his team with military-like precision.

"I was with my boyfriend Cal Perkins when we heard the sirens." I clung to the steering wheel. "I'm so sorry. Your mother-in-law was a dear friend of mine." Fresh tears pricked my eyes.

"Mine too." Earl leaned forward. "And I'm very sorry. She was a fine lady."

"I can't believe it." Jack rubbed the back of his thick neck. "Denise has been telling her mom for years that she needed to get a security system." He lowered his voice. "We came to pick up Clara, but Denise is so upset that she isn't exactly itching to get out and face her long-lost sister." He glanced back at his truck.

Had Denise and Jack gotten back together? Or had they just called a truce during this tragedy?

The woman in the deputy's car at the end of the driveway got out and picked her way toward us. "Jack?"

The Jeep's headlights illuminated her mascara-streaked face. Snowflakes accumulated on her artificial black hair that gave her a hardened look and aged her beyond her fifty-odd years. She crept toward her brother-in-law as if she were afraid of him.

"Clara." He opened his arms and buried her—and the dog—in a hug. "So good to see you again."

Miss Peacock strained toward me, and Clara stepped away from Jack to survey me. "Who are you?"

"Georgia Winston. I live down the road." I motioned over my shoulder. "I'm so sorry for your loss. Your mother meant a lot to me."

Understanding dawned in her expression. "Ray Winston's daughter." Her sweeping gaze and icy tone chilled my already freezing body while Miss Peacock whined.

"Yes, ma'am." I dropped my hands into my lap.

"Nosy, just like that good-for-nothing father of yours."

I winced and pressed my hands together.

"If Ray hadn't snooped around Dad's elevator that night, he wouldn't have gotten himself killed." She secured Miss Peacock under her arm, leaned into the Jeep, and shook her fist in my face. "The stress of Ray's death put my dad in an early grave."

Whoa. That was the first I'd heard this version of the story, but I wasn't about to argue with a self-defense instructor whose fist was close enough to do serious damage to my noggin.

I leaned toward Earl and held up my hands in surrender. "Ma'am, I'm sorry I upset you. Earl and I will be on our way."

After crying myself to sleep—something I didn't do often—I awoke with a start around four in the morning. Blinking my raw eyes, I padded into the living room, flicked the backyard spotlights on, and pushed the curtains aside. Guard-dog Gus's snores drifted in from the laundry room where he slept on the bed in his crate.

The snow continued to fall steadily, and judging from the fact that the fresh blanket was level with the step on my back porch, I'd say the eight-to-ten-inches predicted would end up being accurate. I dropped the curtain back in place and returned to my room.

My gaze fell on the manila envelope sticking out of my purse on the chair in the corner. I grabbed the envelope and went back to my living room where I curled up in Daddy's old leather recliner and spread Grandma Winston's crocheted blanket over my feet.

I shuffled through pictures of Daddy in high school—grainy photos of him in his football jersey. He'd always been proud that his team had won the state championship during his sophomore year. To this day, it was still the only state title our small high school could boast about.

There was even a program from the thirtieth anniversary reunion of the state championship. The Wildcat Springs History Museum had sponsored a dinner on homecoming weekend, and Daddy had served on the planning committee with Beverly, Earl Smith, Jack Schultz, Wanda Morris, Fiona Sylvan, and a few other people whose names I didn't recognize. I slid the program back in the envelope and moved on to the pictures.

I giggled at the faded snapshot of Daddy at prom—with Clara Alspaugh. But hadn't he gone with Mom? They'd been high school sweethearts. I flipped it over and found the date written in faded blue ink. May 10, 1980. His junior year. Mom and Dad hadn't starting dating until his senior year.

Interesting.

Clara's hair was a natural brown, and her eyes held a spark of fun. A pink rose wrist corsage with a silver ribbon complemented her puffy-sleeved, teal dress. I'd seen pictures of Beverly in her younger years, and Clara looked a lot like her mother. What had made Clara want to run away from her hometown? And what had drawn her back?

Her accusation still shocked me. I'd never had a single hint from Beverly that anyone in her family blamed Daddy's situation for her husband Bill's sudden death.

With a sigh, I put the envelope on the end table and pulled my blanket to my chin. For years after Daddy's murder, I'd searched for his killer and encountered one dead-end after another. Finally, God showed me that my quest was robbing me of joy and asked me to stop looking. Even though it'd been one of the hardest things I'd ever done, I quit. After I met Cal back in October, he promised to look at Daddy's case with a fresh perspective, since he hadn't been one of the original detectives on the investigation. But his workload had hindered his progress.

I squeezed my eyes shut. Beverly's family might never have answers about who murdered their loved one—and that was an experience I wouldn't wish on anyone.

CHAPTER THREE

"How're you doing?" Cal asked later that morning.

I put my phone on speaker and set it on the truck's hood. I was bundled up in my blue Carhartt overalls and coat, attaching my snowplow to my truck in the pole barn that housed some of my tractors and farm equipment. The snow had stopped, and now it was time to start digging out.

"Pretty shaken up," I said. "I'll be plowing out my friends to keep busy."

"I get it. I'm having a hard time with this too."

I bent over and attached the electrical cable, so I'd be able to maneuver the plow with the controller in my truck cab. "Do you really think this was a robbery gone wrong?"

"Seems to be." There was no mistaking the hint of doubt in his tone.

I straightened. "Was anything missing?" My gray-striped cat jumped off the tool bench in the corner, padded across the concrete, and rubbed his head against my leg. I bent and stroked his head.

"Denise confirmed Beverly stopped at the bank's walk-up

ATM and withdrew a thousand dollars in cash yesterday after they had brunch at Velda's Café. Says it wasn't that unusual for her mom to take out that much money at a time. Denise doesn't think anything else is missing from the house."

I squeezed my eyes shut. "Beverly was killed over a thousand dollars?" Not that any amount would've been okay.

"Possibly. It makes me sick too. The teens Earl Smith reported driving by could've seen her at the ATM earlier that day and thought they could get their hands on some easy drug money since she lives alone."

I chewed my lip, picked up my phone, and paced in front of my truck. "That makes sense. Clara isn't a suspect, is she?"

"All I can say is that the evidence supports the events she described."

I walked over to the barn door to peek out—no plows had cleared the road. "What if somebody was after Clara, and Beverly got in the way?" Goosebumps rose on my arms as I shut out the cold air.

"What makes you say that?"

"Clara's car was in the driveway, so they should've concluded Beverly wasn't alone. If I were targeting a widow who lived by herself, I'd wait until she didn't have a guest."

"Good point, but the person could've assumed it was Beverly's car. Denise picked her mother up the day she withdrew the money. Besides, someone who needs a fix isn't thinking rationally."

Tears flooded my eyes, and I dug a tissue from my pocket. "You're probably right." I dabbed my eyes. It was a good thing I hadn't bothered with mascara.

"Vanessa and I aren't finished digging." He sighed. "I have to go. Hang in there. I'll see you tonight."

The county plow trucks finally made it by my house, but it took some work pushing snow before I could escape my own driveway. It was after lunch when I headed to my best friend Ashley Choi's bungalow across from Sycamore Park in Wildcat Springs.

It didn't take long to clear her short driveway, and when I finished, my petite friend came outside through her garage, bundled up as if she were about to hit the slopes in Aspen. Two dark braids peeked out from under her fuzzy lavender hat. She toted a shovel, which she waved at me.

I put the truck in park and opened the window. "I don't do sidewalks."

"I know." She rolled her eyes. "Why don't I live in Florida?"

"Because you love your friends so much, and our town is quaint and charming." Except for the part where people were murdered with stunning frequency.

"How was your birthday, hon?" She was always calling people *sweetie* or *hon* in her Kentucky drawl.

"Nice. Until Beverly Alspaugh was murdered." Saying the words brought a lump to my throat, and my nose burned.

"What?" Her jaw dropped. "How?"

"Someone broke into her house and shot her."

"That's awful." She stabbed the shovel into the snow and held on. "Are you okay?" Her dark eyes were full of sympathy.

"Mostly." I stiffened.

"Do you want to come in for some hot chocolate and talk about it?"

"Not today." I shook my head. "Another time. I need to keep moving. I haven't been to Heather's or Brandi's yet."

"Okay." Ashley wrapped her arms around her waist. "Does Cal have any leads?"

"He and his new partner think Beverly interrupted a robbery."

"Oh, hon that's like—"

"I know." I shook my head and looked away.

"Are you *sure* you don't want to come in? I'd be happy to listen."

"Yeah. I'm sure." I studied her. "Is something on your mind? Because normally you wave through the window when I'm pushing snow."

She opened her mouth but then snapped it shut. "It can wait." She stood on her tiptoes and gripped the edge of the door with both hands, revealing her red snowflake mittens.

"But you came out here to tell me, and I need something else to think about." I smiled. "So out with it."

She bit her lip and looked away. "J.T. asked me out on a date."

I did a mental happy jig that my cousin had finally made a move. "And?"

"I said I'd think about it."

"What's to think about?" I stifled a groan and leaned back against the headrest. J.T. had been crushing on Ashley for months —though she didn't know because I was sworn to secrecy. "You'd be great together."

"Maybe. But things have been crazy at work, and I'm not sure I'm ready for something that could get serious."

"I understand. But you sound like Brandi and me—before we started dating our guys."

"The Excuse Queens. Yeah, I know, hon."

Boy-crazy Ashley had recently told Brandi and me about her broken engagement—though we'd known her for going on three years, since she'd moved here from Louisville. In spite of going on a lot of dates, she was reluctant to trust a man enough to develop a serious relationship.

"What'd he say when you told him you'd think about it?"

"He said that was cool."

"Did he look upset?"

"We were texting, but his texts didn't *seem* like he was disappointed."

Because text message tone was so easy to decipher. I put a restraining order on my burgeoning eye roll.

She tugged on her coat. "I don't want to ruin my friendship with him. Do you know how awkward things would be at Bible study if we pursued this and it didn't work out? One of us would have to drop out. The group could split." She rested her forehead on her hands. "You'd have to pick his side over mine because you're family."

I resisted the urge to bang my head against the steering wheel. "Just because you go out a few times doesn't mean the relationship will end in disaster. You might both decide that being friends is best. You're overthinking this."

"No. I'm thinking for the first time—when it comes to relationships." She met my gaze, and there was no mistaking the turmoil in her eyes.

I put my hand on top of her mitten. "Then I'll pray that God shows you the right decision."

"Thanks." She relaxed her death grip on my truck door. "And I'll definitely be praying about the Beverly situation."

When I arrived at Brandi Hartfield's brick split-level house in the Sycamore Hills subdivision, she already had her sidewalk shoveled, and she rushed out the front door with a foil-covered paper plate.

I opened the window. "Are you enjoying your snow day?"

Brandi taught eighth grade social studies at Wildcat Springs Junior High.

"Always. Except now that we have e-learning, I have to grade the assignments my students are turning in. But it beats adding on days at the end of the year." She thrust the plate at me. "Double chocolate cookies. Fresh from the oven."

"Yes!" I pumped my fist. I was always happy to accept cookies as payment—not that anything was necessary for me to help my friends. I slipped a cookie from under the foil and took a bite. The chocolate was still gooey. "This is so good."

"Thanks." She adjusted the red sock cap that'd belonged to her late husband, and her expression turned serious. "I just read the prayer chain email about Beverly." She grimaced. "It makes me sick. She was such a wonderful lady. You doing okay?"

"Mostly." I unlocked the door. "Hop in."

She picked her way to the passenger side, got in the truck, and while I carefully moved the snow to the right side of her driveway, I filled her in on everything that'd happened the night before—including Clara looking like she wanted to beat me senseless.

Brandi's motherly tendencies made it easy to confide in her. Plus, she was seven years older than me and had been through a difficult time when she'd lost her husband Brian in a car accident three years ago.

"What does Cal think?" Brandi tugged off her sock cap and fluffed her flattened brown curls.

I used the plow to backdrag some snow away from her garage door and then pushed the snow to the growing pile. "I'm not sure. Right now, they're pursuing the robbery-gone-wrong angle. At least that's what I got from our last conversation. He's being careful what he says, and he obviously can't share everything."

"Which drives you crazy."

"A little, but I understand." I took my time removing the remaining snow from her garage and shoving it into the pile. When I finished and glanced back at her, a pained expression had settled on her face. "What's wrong?"

Brandi chewed her lip. "I haven't told you this because I

31

didn't want to gossip, but now that Beverly's been killed, it might be relevant."

I put the truck in park. "What?" If Brandi was willing to spill, then it *had* to be important, because she hated gossip.

"I stopped by the Wildcat Springs Museum last Wednesday afternoon to schedule a time to bring my history club students over to see the new exhibit about the high school's athletic department." She twisted her sock cap. "I overheard Beverly talking to someone back in the office, and she sounded upset."

"Who was she talking to?"

"I couldn't tell."

"What was she saying?"

Brandi squinted. "Something like 'I'm not sure you can keep this a secret much longer. I'll keep my mouth shut, but you know how certain people in this town love to gossip.'"

My mouth dropped. Brandi *never* passed along anything this juicy. "Did the other person say anything?"

"No. I thought Beverly was on the phone until she said, 'Wait. Don't go!' A door slammed. I ran outside to look down the alley at the side exit, but the dumpster blocked my view. By the time I got around it, whoever it was had vanished. I'm guessing the mystery person parked in the United Methodist lot and went out the church's driveway. Since they left through the back, I wonder if it was another volunteer."

I stared at my best friend. "Brandi Renee Hartfield. I'm rubbing off on you."

She crossed her arms. "No. You're not."

"If you say so. But I'm impressed with your fine detective work. Cal needs to hear about this."

"I know. I left a message for him as soon as I got the email about Beverly."

I tapped my thumb against the steering wheel. "When I'm done plowing for Heather, I'll go see Wanda. Beverly might've confided in her about any conflicts between the volunteers, since she works there too."

Brandi raised her eyebrows. "Unless . . ."

"What?"

"What if Wanda's the mystery person?"

My eyes widened. "Seriously?" I didn't like what Brandi was implying.

"Maybe it's nothing. But if you start nosing around, things could get awkward with your family. Let Cal handle the case."

I turned down the heat and unzipped my coat. "Wanda shouldn't be offended if I tread carefully. Besides, even if she *is* the mystery person, she didn't kill Beverly."

Brandi brushed a smudge of dust from her jeans.

"Wait. You think Wanda might've killed Beverly?" My voice launched into chipmunk territory. "You've got to be kidding."

I followed her gaze as she looked out the window. The neighbor boys were building a fort between pelting each other with snowballs.

"I highly doubt it," she said softly.

Her gentle tone did little to reassure me. *But . . .*

"But how well do you know Wanda?" She met my eyes.

"You're suggesting an elderly woman staged a break-in at her friend's house, stole her money, and shot her. Over what?" Wanda was an energetic seventy-six with longevity in her genes, thanks to a mother who'd died last year at the age of one hundred, but this was absurd. Brandi was usually more sensible than this.

"That does sound far-fetched, but how well do you know her?"

I huffed. "Fine. Not very well. When she was the high school nurse, I visited her office maybe one time. She and Grandpa haven't dated that long, but he's known her since high school." I tapped my thumb against the steering wheel. "She's a sweet lady and one of Beverly's best friends."

"You're right." Brandi shoved her sock cap into her pocket. "I know better than to speculate. I don't know what got into me." She opened the door. "I'm really sorry. Forget I said anything." She hopped out of the truck and waved as she entered her house.

With the uneasiness settling in my gut, forgetting wouldn't be easy. What if Wanda *wasn't* the nice woman we believed she was?

Before I headed to Heather's house, I decided some coffee from Latte Conspiracies was in order, because it'd be perfect with Brandi's cookies. Not to mention, the shop's owner, Bobbi Sue Miller, always knew your business before you did, and she'd been an excellent source in the past. Though, I wasn't sure how much gossip she could've heard with the snow keeping everyone hunkered down.

Sure enough, there wasn't much activity in downtown Wildcat Springs, though the streets had been cleared. Unlike a regular day, I had my choice of parking spaces close to the entrance. I pulled in beside a black Escape emblazoned with a logo for a visiting nurse service.

When I entered the coffee shop, the bell jingled, and my eyes fell on the lone, gray-haired woman sitting at one of the tables facing the brick wall.

I stuffed my gloves in my overall pockets and approached the stainless-steel counter. Bobbi Sue's lanky—but handsome—son Hamlet appeared from the back room. I'd heard that he'd recently returned to Wildcat Springs after spending several years acting in theater productions. Now he was planning a house-flipping career.

"Good day, Georgia Rae." Hamlet had a thing for sweater vests, and I swear he had one for every day of the winter months.

He'd worn them since high school, when he'd been my brother Dakota's best friend.

"Hey. How're you doing?"

His blue-gray eyes sparkled as he puffed out his argyle-bedecked chest. "Excellent—now that you're here." His deep voice held a note of admiration. "What can I get for you?"

I glanced at the clipboards that held the specialty drinks' descriptions. "Large dark roast coffee—to go." It was a departure from my usual order, but I wasn't in the mood for a Moon Landing Mocha, an Area 51 Latte, or a Crop Circle Cappuccino. "What's new in your world?"

"I've decided to move back to Wildcat Springs permanently since my girlfriend and I parted company." He rang up my order.

"I'm sorry. But it's nice to have you back in town." He'd been based in Chicago for the last four years.

"Thanks. I bought the old Williams place out on 900 East. It needs a lot of work, but I don't mind." He took the money I held out and punched my loyalty card.

"Keep the change."

"Thanks." He dumped it in the tip jar next to the cash register. "My ex is a nice person, but we weren't compatible. She wasn't willing to move to Wildcat Springs since she loves city life, and this Hamlet prefers hamlets." He grabbed a cup and poured my coffee.

"To thine own self be true." The edge of my mouth twitched as our eyes met.

"Exactly." He winked and slid my coffee across the counter.

I should quit encouraging him, because he'd had a major crush on me back in the day. I glanced around the shop. "Is your mom here?"

"No. She and Dad left yesterday morning on a ten-day Caribbean cruise for their anniversary."

I stifled a sigh. "Good for them. My mom and stepdad are in Hawaii. I'm jealous of anyone who gets to escape winter."

"Same here. But someone has to hold down the fort." He pointed to the doors that led to Miller's Books, the shop his dad Hemingway ran. "I kept the bookstore closed but thought our town's denizens might need coffee." He nodded at the woman who was typing on a laptop. "You and that lady are the only ones who've come in."

From my current angle, I got a better look at the woman. It was Beverly's other daughter, Denise Schultz. I took that as a sign from the Almighty that I needed to speak with the woman. "Thanks, Hamlet."

"Wait." He darted around the counter and blocked my path to Denise. "Are you still dating Detective Perkins?"

"Yes."

He tilted his head. "You're not engaged, are you?"

"N-no." The intensity in his chiseled face unnerved me and sent the teeniest, tiniest ripple through my stomach. What was wrong with me? "We've only been dating a few months." I shoved my hands in my pockets and studied my snow boots.

"If I were him, I'd have sealed the deal by now."

My face flamed as I looked at Hamlet. "Why? There's no point in rushing things. It makes sense to get to know each other, and I've never understood people who meet someone and just up and get married so quickly." I threw my hands up. "What if that person turns out to be a serial killer? How can you be sure? Didn't it take you a while to figure out your ex-girlfriend wasn't the right one for you? Not that she's a Lizzie Borden, and it's not that Cal's an ax murderer, because he's one of the good guys . . . but . . . but . . ."

Why, oh why, wasn't he stopping me? I took a deep breath and tried to read Hamlet's inscrutable expression.

He simply walked back behind the counter, picked up a rag,

and swiped the stainless-steel surface. "I didn't mean to upset you. I've heard good things about Detective Perkins, so I don't think you need to worry." He smiled. "See you later, Georgia Rae."

"See ya." Holding onto my coffee cup for dear life, I whirled around and marched to Denise's table.

Unlike her sister Clara, Denise hadn't ventured from Wildcat Springs. She'd married, had a son and daughter, and worked as a home healthcare nurse.

"Denise?"

She stopped typing, removed her reading glasses, and looked up. "Hello, there." Her splotchy skin and puffy eyes advertised her grief.

"I'm so sorry about your mom. I thought the world of her."

She motioned for me to have a seat. "She thought a lot of you too." She closed her laptop, folded her glasses, and set them on the table. "I had to get out of my house. I'm writing Mama's obituary, though I doubt my sister will approve." She grimaced and closed her beige cardigan. "I heard about how Clara snapped at you last night. I'm sorry."

"It's okay." I waved my hand. "Clara was in shock. It had to be terrible, coming home after all this time and . . ." I didn't want to think about Beverly's death, let alone say the words.

"Yes. It is." She folded her arms across her chest. "But Clara chose to stay away."

"Why?"

She flinched. "I thought you, of all people, would know that."

The prom picture of Daddy and Clara together loomed in my memory, and a wave of heat made my overalls and coat feel suffocating. "But I don't." I unzipped my jacket.

She folded her hands and met my gaze. "Your dad broke my sister's heart."

CHAPTER FOUR

"I'm sorry." I twisted the alien-print cardboard ring circling my coffee cup.

"Why are *you* apologizing?" Denise took a drink of coffee from an oversized, lime-colored mug.

"Because Daddy can't?" Winstons were incredibly loyal.

"That's sweet." Denise chuckled and set her mug on the table. "I didn't tell you this to make you feel bad. I figured you'd probably heard your family talk about it."

I thought of Daddy and Clara's prom picture. Clara had looked so happy, but hadn't she clung to Daddy's arm possessively? "I knew Daddy and Clara went to prom together."

"Yep. They broke up after that. My sister should've bounced back since she had a lot going for her. Not to mention a bunch of other guys wanted to date her."

"What happened?"

She shrugged. "I don't know details. I was away at college, and Clara certainly never told me. All I know is that things went bad between Clara and your dad right around prom time, and the day after graduation, she left town and swore she'd never be back.

Your dad still had a year of high school and, as I'm sure you know, that's when he started dating your mom."

I tried to make sense of everything Denise was telling me. "But Daddy's been gone for over nine years. If he was what was keeping your sister away, then why didn't she come back for your dad's funeral?"

Denise set her jaw. "Because I told her not to. She had no right to stay away for years and then come waltzing back for Dad's funeral. He would've *loved* for her to visit when she was alive, but she never made the effort. When Mom and Dad did go to Texas, she always made them feel like they were in the way." She pressed her lips together. "Mom and I didn't need the added drama. It was upsetting enough dealing with Dad's sudden death."

Wow. "Denise, if I ask you something, will you be completely honest with me?"

"Sure. Unless you want me to tell you how much I weigh—in which case I'll have to lie." She didn't crack a smile.

Okay, then. With her slim figure, the number couldn't possibly have been embarrassing, but whatever.

"Last night, Clara said your dad died from worrying about my dad's murder—that your dad blamed himself. Is that true?"

She stared out at the street. "Dad died when it was his time. He felt awful about Ray's killer going free, because he figured if he'd had security cameras at the elevator, then the detectives would've solved the case. He talked about getting cameras, because of vandalism and thieves stealing grain but never got around to it. I think he never thought anything bad would happen in Wildcat Springs." Denise tossed a napkin over a puddle of coffee on the table, and the liquid bled into the paper. "Clara's absence played more of a role in Dad's death than anything. She's just trying to make herself feel better by shifting blame. Don't let her."

I nodded. The muffled, chiming melody of "How Firm a Foundation" filtered in from the United Methodist Church's bell tower across the street. "One more thing."

"Yes?"

"Other than Clara coming home, was there anything your mother was worried or upset about recently?"

"Not that I'm aware of." She didn't meet my gaze and brushed non-existent crumbs from the table.

Had Denise been the one arguing with Beverly at the museum? Could the conversation have had something to do with her separation from Jack?

"I take it you aren't buying the teenagers-looking-for-drug money theory." A pained expression flitted over her features.

"I'm not sure what to think."

"I completely understand." She bowed her head.

"I'm sorry." I stood and rested my hand on her shoulder. "I didn't mean to upset you."

She met my eyes. "No. You didn't say anything I hadn't already thought of."

Did she suspect her own sister had shot their mother and staged the scene? I had to bite my tongue to keep from asking because there had to be a better way to find out. "I'll let you get back to writing. I have one more friend I need to plow out. Thanks for your time." I turned to leave.

"Georgia?"

I faced her. "Yeah?"

Denise swallowed. "Don't let Clara make you feel like you can't come to Mom's funeral."

I hadn't thought that far ahead. "Thank you."

"No. Thank *you* for always being so good to Mama."

Tears pricked my eyes. "You're welcome."

After they'd become engaged, Grandpa and Wanda had purchased a condo outside of Wildcat Springs. Wanda had already sold her house and moved in, and Grandpa planned to join her after the wedding.

When I finished clearing Heather's driveway, I drove to the sea of copy-and-paste condos that surrounded a large pond. The maintenance crew had already made the rounds, so the driveways and streets were passable.

I double-checked the house numbers, but knew I had the right place when I spotted Wanda's snow-covered black Camry parked in the driveway and the silver gazing ball adorned with a ceramic cardinal.

Wanda loved birds.

There was no mistaking the surprise that flitted through her expression when she swung the door open. "Come on in, Georgia." She ushered me into the living room, which held a couch, recliner, TV, and a dozen or so boxes stacked in the corner. The smell of simmering hamburger and onions filled the cozy space.

"If I'd known you had so much unpacking to do, I would've volunteered to help." I pointed to the containers we'd lugged in two weeks ago.

Wanda shrugged. "Don't worry about it. The garage is full of boxes too, but my kitchen is set up, which is all I'm worried about right now. Most of these are full of keepsakes and knickknacks, but your grandpa has some packing to do if you have time to help this week."

"Sure. I'll see what I can do."

She pointed toward the kitchen. "I'm working on some chili for supper, and I need to check on the hamburger."

"No problem." I followed her to the kitchen and perched on the stool at the small island.

"Want something to drink?"

"Water would be great, please." My eyes fell on a manila

envelope sitting on the granite counter. Wanda's name was written in Beverly's handwriting. "I see Beverly gave you some pictures too."

"Yes. She gave them to me yesterday afternoon, but I haven't looked through them yet." She blinked back tears and grabbed a water bottle from the refrigerator, which was covered in family pictures held in place by souvenir magnets from her travels all over the United States. "I can't believe she's gone." She set the bottle in front of me.

"Same here."

"What do you think about the interrupted break-in story?" She turned to the stove to stir the meat.

Since Wanda had been known to repeat everything she knew, I treaded carefully. "I'm not sure. It's weird that Clara stayed away for thirty-eight years, and right when she showed up, her mom got killed."

Wanda furrowed her brow as she opened a can of tomato juice. "Yes." She dumped the juice into the pot and stirred. "It doesn't sit right with me either. What's your boyfriend think?"

"He never says much about his cases, but I think they're pursuing the break-in angle." I took a sip of water and considered the best way to frame my next question. "Did Beverly seem out of sorts about anything lately?"

"Not that I observed. She was apprehensive about seeing Clara again, but that was all she shared with me." She pointed at the manila envelope sitting next to me. "Go ahead and open that. I want to see what Bev put in there."

I picked it up, and resting underneath, was an envelope from the National Rifle Association.

Interesting.

"Are you an NRA member?" My stomach twisted as I held up the envelope.

"Yep. My late husband had quite a collection of firearms, but

I sold them when I moved here. Paul and I used to practice shooting like some couples play golf." Wanda removed a can of tomato sauce from her pantry.

Perfectly legal, right? Brandi owned a gun and even had a permit to carry it. I took a sip of water. "Do you and grandpa ever go to the shooting range?"

"No, Ron would rather be bowling, but I went last week. I've got to keep my skills sharp." She looked me straight in the eyes. "If someone breaks into *my* house, they're going to be greeted by my Glock 19."

"Good for you." I didn't quite achieve the casual tone I'd been going for. I slid the pictures out of the envelope. "Speaking of bowling. How'd Grandpa's league tournament go last night?" No sense in making her feel like a suspect, but verifying she had an alibi would go a long way toward making *me* feel better.

Her face fell. "I forgot to ask him this morning. I didn't end up going, because I had some wedding things to take care of, and I went to bed before the tournament was over."

In other words, Grandpa wasn't her alibi.

"I'm sure he understands," I said. "Were you busy working on decorations?"

"No." She turned her attention to the chili. "So, who's in the pictures?"

Okay, then. Life Lesson #201: Never stir up trouble.

Telling myself she'd probably been lingerie shopping and didn't want to discuss the matter with me, I shuffled through the stack and stopped when I ran across a picture of Wanda sitting on a couch next to her first husband Paul. He was a nice-looking man with a square jaw. Both of them wore cowboy hats, boots, and matching blue flannel shirts. I flipped the picture over. The date was 2007. Paul had died three years ago from pancreatic cancer.

"Nice costumes." I held it up.

She leaned over to look at the picture. "Bev took that at a Wild West Sunday school party she and Bill hosted." She chuckled. "Beverly knew how to throw a good shindig in her day." Her smile faded. "Everyone loved her."

Maybe not everyone. I tucked the pictures away. "So Beverly never had any conflicts with anybody at church?"

"No."

"What about problems with the museum volunteers?"

"Not that I'm aware of." She turned and selected a seasoning packet from her cabinet.

"Did she ever say why Clara decided to come home?"

"She wanted to make amends. Wasn't an issue with needing money—Beverly said she made that clear right away." She ripped open a seasoning packet and sprinkled it into the pot. "She didn't say a lot about Clara. Why would she?"

"True. What about Denise?"

"Oh, Beverly talked about Denise all the time—they were very close. They got along great."

I traced my finger over the crease in the water bottle. "I heard Denise and her husband are having marriage trouble."

"Yes, but I don't know any details since Beverly never said." Wanda crumpled the packet and tossed it into the trash. "I never understood why Denise married Jack Schultz. He was a jerk when he was young, and he hasn't changed. Not to mention, he never got along with Beverly—or Bill when he was alive." She shook her finger at me. "If or when you and that boyfriend of yours ever decide to tie the knot, don't be thinking you're gonna change him."

"I know." I liked Cal the way he was, and I hoped he'd say the same about me.

"And if you marry somebody, you marry his family, so you'd better like them too."

"Excellent advice." I raised my eyebrows. "I take it that means you like us?"

"Sure do. I know I'm getting a stubborn old coot for a husband. But I love him, and I can put up with it because he's so good to me."

I laughed. "Stubbornness runs in the Winston family."

"Sure does." Her eyes sparkled.

"Back to Clara for a minute." I relayed to Wanda everything Clara had said about Daddy. "It's hard to believe she's so bitter after almost forty years."

Wanda drained a can of kidney beans in the sink and pressed her lips together.

Uh-oh. "There's something else, isn't there?"

Silence fell over the kitchen as she rinsed and added the beans to her chili. "Look." She faced me. "I understand you have questions about Clara, but I'm not convinced there's anything else you need to know."

I closed my eyes. The way she said it made me wonder about Daddy's involvement. "Wanda, don't leave me hanging like that." Why was she choosing this opportunity to be discreet?

"It's best if I do." She adjusted the burner's temperature. "If you want answers about your dad and Clara, talk to your mother."

CHAPTER FIVE

E ven though I was in my four-wheel drive truck, I took it easy on the slick country roads while fighting my lead foot. I was running behind because after I'd left Wanda's condo, I'd been heading through town when a widow from my church called and asked me to dig her out since her son was in Jamaica.

This served to bolster my conviction that half of Richard County had taken refuge near the equator.

I'd already decided the conversation with my mom would have to wait because she and Dan wouldn't be home from Hawaii until late Saturday night, and my gut told me it'd be best to chat about Daddy's teenage drama in person. Right now, I turned my focus to making myself look cute—ASAP—because Cal was bringing Chinese take-out.

When I turned into the driveway, a red hatchback blocked the side of the garage where I normally parked my truck.

Clara Alspaugh. What in the world?

I stopped on the cement approach, and she got out of her car. Nothing in her body language suggested she was as angry as she'd been the night before, but I made sure my phone was easily accessible in my overall pocket.

Help me be kind, Lord. I took a deep breath, tapped my garage door opener, and slid out of my truck.

"Hi, Clara." I forced myself to sound pleasant, but my voice came out like a perky cheerleader who'd sucked a helium balloon. "Do you want to come in?" I motioned toward the house.

She shook her head. "This won't take long." Her bloodshot eyes were rimmed with dark circles. "I owe you an apology and an explanation for overreacting last night." She studied her multi-colored athletic shoes.

"It's okay. You were in shock. I'm sorry my daddy's death caused your father so much stress."

"Dad had a weak heart—for years. Mama would be ashamed if she knew I lashed out at you like that." She fidgeted with the zipper on her red fleece jacket. "Truth is, I loved your dad so much that it was hard seeing his girl. Especially when I don't have any children of my own."

I bit my lip. "I'm sorry."

"It's not your fault." She smoothed her hair and gazed out toward the grain bins that stood next to my pole barn.

Seconds ticked by as the frigid wind whipped around us, and I opened my mouth to fill the silence with some Georgia-style jabbering, but instead, I whispered, "Your mom was so glad you were coming home."

Tears filled her eyes. "You know the prodigal's father in the Bible? That's how it was. When I arrived on Thursday night, she welcomed me with open arms and chicken and noodles—my favorite meal. We had a wonderful talk before we went to bed. And then . . ." She dabbed her eyes with her coat sleeve.

Her genuine emotion poked holes in my theory that she'd shot her mother and staged the scene, but while she was here, I figured I should keep her talking. "Why'd you leave Wildcat Springs?"

She hung her head. "I thought my life would be better if I got out of this town." Clara shoved her hands in her coat pockets and looked me in the eyes. "I could never measure up to my big sister Denise because she was Mama and Dad's favorite. The pretty cheerleader with the quarterback boyfriend. A walking cliché. Plus, Ray was never going to leave because he wanted to farm with his dad."

"Did you and Daddy break up over that?" Clara's story wasn't sounding like the scandal Denise and Wanda had alluded to.

"No. We split because your dad was overprotective of me—at least I thought so at the time—and I resented it. I let my family and friends think the break-up was Ray's fault, but it was all mine. I'm ashamed about that, and I knew if I ever visited, I'd have to face my past." She waved a hand. "It's a long story, and I don't want to get into that ancient history." She moved toward her car. "I'd best be on my way. You have more important things to do than listening to me reliving the past. I just wanted to apologize."

Even though I wasn't satisfied with her answer about Daddy, I couldn't let her leave without asking one more question. "Clara, do you think your mom interrupted a teenager looking for drug money, or is there more to it?"

She opened her car door and rested her arm on it. "I've heard how you've solved a couple of murders."

"I helped." There was no sense in taking all of the credit when Cal had done his part in the investigations.

"Since you brought it up, I want your take on something."

"Okay."

Clara swiped her bangs out of her eyes. "I grew up in that old farmhouse, and my sister Denise doesn't walk—she stomps.

When we were kids, every time she was upstairs and I was down, I could hear her pounding around. I never figured out how someone so skinny made so much noise. Part of it was the house's poor insulation and not just her Bigfoot gait."

I tried to make sense of what she was telling me. "The intruder heard you upstairs."

"Yep. I heard the gunshot and leaped out of bed. I weigh a whole lot more now than my sister did as a teenager, and my bedroom's right above the kitchen. The shooter had to have heard my feet hit the floor."

I remembered what Cal had told Detective Hawk last night. "And that person came upstairs after you."

"Right. If you were a thief looking for money and you'd shot a person who'd surprised you, would you take the time to go upstairs and shoot a second person or would you run out to escape?"

"I'd cut my losses and scram."

"Exactly."

"Did you see the getaway car?"

"No. I was too busy taking care of Mama."

I shivered and wrapped my arms around my waist. "Is there anybody in your life who would've been angry enough to try to kill you?"

"My ex-boyfriend hates my guts, but he's in prison for dealing heroin." She flattened her lips.

Interesting. What kind of life had Clara led? "Could he have hired someone to come after you?"

"It's possible, but a professional wouldn't have botched the job. I've replayed last night over and over in my head. The intruder knew how to shoot but was tactically weak. Besides, if it was my ex hiring a hitman, why not have him take me out in Texas where I live alone?"

"True." It seemed surreal to be discussing a hitman. What

had happened to my peaceful small-town life? "What else can you tell me about the shooter?"

"The person was average build and could've been an average-sized man or a tallish woman. Definitely not as tall as you."

I stifled a wry laugh. "I heard you clipped the shooter's coat."

"Sure did. It was a black puffy coat, and the shooter also had on a mask. At first, I assumed the intruder was male, but I wonder if it was a woman trying to hide her figure."

I dug my boot toe into the ground and tried to ignore Gus. He'd heard us talking and was howling as if he were auditioning for a starring role in a musical because I hadn't released him from his crate.

Clara looked toward my back door. "Is your dog okay?"

"He'll survive." My appendages were numbing, and I wanted to ask her to come in but was afraid of ending our conversation prematurely. Instead, I dug in my pockets for my gloves but only found one. *Great.* "Let's put aside the theory that the killer was after you and focus on your mom." I told her what Brandi had overheard at the museum. "Do you have any idea what that could've been about?"

Clara blinked. "Is your friend sure about what Mama said?"

"Yes." I trusted Brandi completely, even though her speculation about Wanda had annoyed me.

"I might have an idea, but it's just a theory."

"What's that?" I tried to keep the impatience out of my voice, but I wasn't 100 percent successful.

"My brother-in-law Jack cheated on Denise with Fiona Sylvan. What if Mama was talking to him?"

CHAPTER SIX

"Does Denise know about Jack's affair with Fiona?" I asked Clara.

Fiona owned Sassy Salon where I had my hair trimmed on a semi-regular basis.

"I don't know. Probably. Since she and Jack are separated," Clara said.

Even though Beverly had already told me this, I still wondered about something. "But they were together last night when they came to pick you up."

"True. But he dropped us off at their house and left. Denise must've needed a shoulder to lean on, and I guess he's trying to win her back." She shrugged. "Denise and I didn't get into details."

"That makes sense."

She nodded. "What if Mama heard something and was giving Jack a chance to come clean instead of telling Denise herself—or before someone else did?" Clara ran her hand back and forth over the top of the car door.

I reconsidered Beverly's words about how people in Wildcat

Springs liked to gossip. "That makes sense. How'd you find out about the affair?"

"Fiona Sylvan and I were friends back in high school, and we've kept in touch. When I told her I was coming to visit, the affair came up, but Fiona swore it's over." She got into her car and started the engine. "My family is such a mess. Thanks for listening." She gazed at me. "Your dad would be proud to see you farming."

"Thanks." My brain was swirling with everything I'd learned in the last few minutes.

After Clara drove away, I let a very miffed Gus out of his crate, and I filled his food dish while he was outside. He thundered back into the house and snarfed down his supper.

While I thawed, I quickly flipped through the mail—nothing but junk that I tossed in the trash as my doorbell chimed.

I groaned and glanced at the clock. I'd been counting on at least twenty more minutes to make myself look presentable, especially since I hadn't bothered with putting on makeup that morning. "Uh-oh. Cal's early, little buddy."

Gus ignored me and slurped water. I smoothed my hair as I walked to the door. I hadn't even taken off my overalls, so I hoped Cal liked the disheveled-farmer look. I threw open the door. "Hey . . . Hamlet." I gave myself an F for failing to keep the shock and dismay out of my voice.

He thrust a glove at me. "It fell out of your pocket as you were leaving. I didn't notice while you were at our shop, but I examined our security camera footage to find the owner."

"I didn't know you had cameras." Though it didn't surprise me because Bobbi Sue's paranoia was a town legend. I took my wayward glove.

"Mom had them installed a couple of weeks ago."

"I see." I found it interesting Bobbi Sue had waited so long. "Thanks for delivering it."

"No problem." His eyes twinkled. "I didn't want your hand to get cold."

"That's sweet." A nervous chuckle escaped my throat, and I clung to the edge of the door. "I'd invite you in, but I have plans tonight and need to change." Thank goodness I had a ready-made excuse.

"Of course. I won't keep you." He started to turn but then furrowed his brow. "Your dog got in the trash." He pointed behind me.

I whirled around. "Guster Winston!" I bit back a few naughty words that I should've let fly to scare Hamlet away.

Gus held a used coffee filter in his mouth. He'd left a trail from the kitchen to the foyer, and he wagged his tail and gazed up at me, as if daring me to embark on a chase that would spread grounds all over my house.

A drip of coffee plunked to the floor as I stared down my vengeful dog.

"Hamlet?" I whispered.

"Yes?"

"Do you remember where the utility room is?" My fingers curled around my glove.

"Sure do."

"Will you slip past me and get the dustbuster? It's on the floor in the corner. Gus hates the noise and will drop whatever he's got if you turn it on."

I froze in place and prayed Gus would stay put as Hamlet moved.

"On my way." He darted behind me and down the hall. A few seconds later he charged out, brandishing the dustbuster like a sword.

"Turn it on," I hissed.

As soon as Gus heard the high-pitched whine, he dropped the filter. Unfortunately, he tracked back over his coffee-ground path on the way to his crate and managed to distribute more grounds over my hallway and kitchen floor.

I stuffed my glove in my pocket as I trudged to the kitchen. My shoulders slumped when I saw the overturned trashcan—a cornucopia of waste spilling onto the floor.

I gritted my teeth. "I didn't get the lid shut when I threw away my junk mail," I stomped to the utility room where Gus cowered in his crate. I slammed the door, locked it, and returned to the kitchen, where I skidded on a puddle of coffee.

Hamlet reached for my arm and steadied me.

My face flamed, and I tried to ignore my fluttering stomach. "Thanks."

"Your doggie discipline is very effective." Hamlet let go of my arm, stooped over, and began sweeping the grounds.

"You don't have to do that."

He waved a hand. "It's no trouble." He worked his way toward the foyer.

"Thank you." I righted the overturned can and began tossing the trash inside.

A few minutes later, we'd cleaned up the worst of the coffee chaos, but I'd still need to mop. "Gus has been going through a spiteful phase lately. He doesn't like it when I'm gone for a long time, and I was out plowing for most of the day."

"My family's dog, Scout, used to drag toilet paper all over the house after we'd been gone on vacation." He set the dustbuster on the kitchen table. "It's nice to be loved."

"I guess so." I shoved my hands in my pockets. "Thanks again for your help." We moved to the front door. "And for returning my glove."

"You're very welcome."

Our eyes met long enough to venture into Awkwardland. As I turned away and opened the door, Cal strolled up the porch steps. He held a plastic bag, which I hoped contained our dinner.

"Hey!" My voice was pitched unnaturally high. I stepped aside to let him in, and my stomach growled when I caught a whiff of greasy egg rolls. "Cal, this is Hamlet Miller. Hamlet, this is Detective Cal Perkins—my *boyfriend*."

Cal swept Hamlet with his gaze and extended his hand. "Nice to meet you."

"Likewise." Hamlet surveyed Cal.

"What brings you to the farm tonight?" Cal's tone was casual, but I detected a slight flicker of suspicion in his blue eyes.

"My glove." I yanked it out of my pocket and waved it around. "I stopped by Latte Conspiracies when I was out plowing, and Hamlet was working because Bobbi Sue and Hemi are on a cruise. I dropped it when I left, and Hamlet was nice enough to bring it to me, but then Gus got in my trash, and of all things, got a used coffee filter and spread grounds all over my hallway, Hamlet helped me clean it up, but I still need to mop . . ."

Both men gaped at me. Merciful heavens. Why was I babbling like a kid caught snooping for birthday presents? I hadn't done anything wrong. "Gus needs obedience school . . ."

Smooth, Georgia Rae.

"I'll be on my way." Hamlet's eyes glittered with amusement. "Enjoy your dinner."

Cal closed the door behind Hamlet and took off his coat. "Nice of him to brave slick roads to deliver a glove."

That lovely little factoid had escaped my notice in all of the chaos. "He was my brother's best friend in high school." I stalked to the utility room and found my mop, and Gus rattled around in his crate. "I've known him for years."

"Let me guess. He had a crush on you."

"Maybe. I'm not a mind reader." I faced him and squashed the guilt from my dishonest answer. "That was a long time ago."

Cal took the mop from my hand. "If he didn't then, he does now." He pulled me up against his muscular chest. His lips met mine, and I forgot about Hamlet, coffee grounds, and my unruly pet. "Go change. I'll keep our food warm and clean the floor."

After dinner, Cal put his arm around me as we lounged on my sectional sofa, chatting and enjoying the warmth of my fireplace. "Vanessa and I were talking today, and we thought it might be fun if you and I went on a double date tomorrow night with her and her fiancé."

I drew a throw pillow to my chest. "Cool. What do you have in mind?"

"She has two extra tickets to see *Grease* at the dinner theater in Richardville."

"Perfect! I'd like to get to know her better."

"She said the same thing about you." He ran his fingers through his hair. "We could use a break after this crazy week at work."

"Speaking of work . . ." I gazed at him. "Is there anything else you're allowed to tell me about Beverly's case?" I gave him my very best smile. I was shameless.

"Not really."

I was used to that answer, so I decided to be a good girlfriend and change the subject. "I had an interesting encounter with Clara Alspaugh today."

He sat up straighter. "You're kidding."

"No." I told him about Clara's apology, her suspicions about the break in, and Jack Schultz's affair with Fiona Sylvan.

"I'm glad Clara apologized," he said when I finished.

I stared at him. "That's all you're going to say?"

"What do you want me to say?"

That you've cleared her as a suspect. I fingered the necklace Cal had given me for my birthday. "Never mind. What movie do you want to watch?" I picked up the remote and scrolled through the on-demand movie choices.

"Don't be mad."

"I'm not mad." Mildly irritated, maybe. I knew there were things he couldn't tell me, and about 95 percent of the time, I was cool with that.

Okay, so maybe it was more like 80 percent.

"How reliable is Earl Smith?" he asked.

That was random. I lowered the remote and turned my attention from the list of movies on the TV screen. "I strongly suspect he's behind the rumor that I was moving to Nashville to try and make it as a country singer."

He grinned. "Were you?"

"No way. I don't have the pipes for that. Besides, I hate country music."

"You're missing out."

"Um, no. I'm not." I considered why Cal had brought up my nosy neighbor. "Earl told Vanessa he saw a gray sedan full of teenagers carrying on shortly before the break in. Is that why you're asking?"

"Yes. We talked to Earl again, but he said after he took his dog out, he was inside watching *Gunsmoke* all night and didn't see anything." Cal laced his fingers through mine. "Which is fine, except Vanessa and I both got the feeling he's hiding something."

My eyes widened. "You think he killed Beverly?" He fit Clara's description of an average-sized man.

"With his arthritis, it's highly unlikely."

"True." I thought of how slowly he'd moved the night of Beverly's death. "Do you want me to see if I have any luck talking to Earl?" Though Cal couldn't tell me everything, in the past he'd asked me to pay attention to what folks around town were saying and let him know if I learned anything important.

"Why are you asking?" His eyes gleamed, and his dimple

made an appearance. "You've already made up your mind to track him down first thing tomorrow morning."

"Exactly—and I know right where to find him."

"Surprise, surprise." He kissed the top of my head. "Just tell me what you find out."

Everyone in Wildcat Springs knew Old Man Smith loved cookies. Each morning until the Lord decided to call Earl home, he'd descend upon Pastry Delight between nine and ten o'clock for coffee and three cookies.

Earl, of course, not God. That would be a whole other story and a testament to the quality of the food at Pastry Delight.

The owner, Taryn Anderson, specialized in pies, but she could've sold only cookies and kept her business afloat. After graduating high school with my brother and Hamlet, she'd gone to a fancy culinary school in New York and had come back home to open a shop. She'd taken the best of both worlds—fancy pastries and her down-home flair—and her shop drew people from all over Richard County and beyond.

Saturday morning, I threw on some workout clothes and a sweatshirt and headed into town. Indiana weather could be absolutely ridiculous, and it had set out to maintain its fickle reputation that day. After the snowstorm had dropped a grand total of ten inches on Wildcat Springs, a warm front descended on our neck of the woods, bringing sun and mild temperatures that I appreciated as I walked to the shop.

When I stepped inside, the door entry alert played a tinny version of "Für Elise." Taryn had used pink on the bakery's sacks and boxes and on the store's walls. Her color choice gave off a sugary vibe.

As expected, Old Man Smith sat behind the *USA Today's*

sports section at his usual table and had already devoured one of his three cookies. A gingersnap and an oatmeal raisin cookie remained on his plate.

"Good morning, Taryn." I approached the counter.

"Morning." She smiled and donned plastic serving gloves. "What can I get for you?" Her perky blond topknot wobbled.

I surveyed her display case loaded with cookies, brownies, pies, muffins, cheesecakes, and tarts. Maybe my hankering was for pie since Taryn had a few varieties that she sold by the slice. I certainly wasn't above eating dessert for breakfast. No. I had a fitted dress to squeeze into for the wedding. A cookie was healthier. "One cranberry-oatmeal-pecan cookie and a small coffee."

Oatmeal was nutritious, right?

"Good choice." She reached for the cookie.

"How's business been?"

"Great. I've been swamped lately—and it's not even wedding season yet." She rang up my purchase.

"I'm looking forward to eating your cake at Grandpa's wedding." Wanda had picked a vanilla cake with raspberry filling.

"Thanks. I hope they love the design."

When I'd paid, I strolled over to Earl, who was perusing the *Richard County Gazette's* minimal contents. "Hey, Neighbor. Mind if I join you for a moment?"

"Sure, Miss Georgia." He folded the paper. "You're much more interesting than this old rag."

"I certainly hope so."

He flicked his fingers against the paper. "You wouldn't think that a paper here in flyover country could have a left-wing bias, but somehow even this editor manages to be out of touch with the people in this county." He dropped it on the table.

"That's too bad." I slipped into the chair across from Earl and sipped my coffee. I didn't love politics, but I couldn't disagree with Earl about the paper's slant. I took a bite of cookie. Taryn had to have just baked this batch because it was soft on the inside with a hint of crispness on the outside.

"What's on your mind?" he asked.

I pointed to the cookie. "Right now, this is all I can focus on."

He guffawed so hard that Taryn jumped and turned around to stare at us. Earl pointed at me. "Get this girl another cranberry-oatmeal-pecan cookie. On me."

I raised a hand. "Oh, no. They're wonderful, but I—"

"Nope." Taryn put a cookie in a bag and bustled around the counter. "Earl's my best customer, so he's the boss." She set the package on the table and moved to help the customers who'd arrived.

"Well, if you insist," I said. "Thank you, Earl."

"No problem. Now, I've been coming here for going on five years, and never once have you strolled in here and joined me. In fact, I'm surprised you're up this early. You ain't exactly a morning person in the winter."

My face warmed, and I took a moment to reassure myself that I always kept my blinds tightly closed after dark—and that Earl's house didn't face my bedroom window. "I'm definitely a night owl." I shoved another bite in my mouth.

"I know." He split his oatmeal raisin cookie in thirds. "I'll bet you're investigating, and you're planning to pick my brain." He tapped his temple.

"Maybe."

"I sure wish I could tell you more than I already told those detectives."

"Maybe you can. You told me you got a package of pictures from Beverly that night. Did she seem upset about anything?"

Earl shook his head. "She was friendly, but I didn't stay long because she was making dinner. I suppose she was nervous about seeing Clara, but she didn't say so. I reckon she was worried about Denise too, seeing as how she and Jack are having trouble, but Bev didn't talk about that either. Speaking of Jack." Earl took a bite and chewed for a few seconds before leaning forward. "You know he's a part-time gun dealer, right? Years ago, he set my Becky up with a revolver. I was gone driving a semi all the time, and she wanted something to protect herself."

"Really." I'd never heard about Jack's side hustle. But then, I hated guns. "Are you suggesting Jack might've shot his mother-in-law?" I whispered.

"Can't be sure." He held up both hands. "Far be it from me to make any accusations. I don't know much else about Jack other than he was a high school football star." He leaned back and crossed his arms. "Wanna know something else interesting?"

"Sure."

"Beverly had an appointment to change her will."

"Seriously?" I had to bite my tongue to keep from asking him why he didn't think that was pertinent information to share with Cal.

"Absolutely." He thrust his thumbs toward his chest. "I know what I overheard on Tuesday when I was eating lunch at Pizza Heaven. I ain't senile."

"I didn't mean to suggest you are."

"Aww, Georgia, relax. I'm messing with you." He shoved half of a gingersnap into his mouth. "Bevvy wan Clawa to have huh faahr shah."

Life Lesson #798: Your mother was right. Don't talk with your mouth full.

Thankfully, he swallowed before continuing. "Much as Clara keeping her distance hurt Bev, she wanted her daughter to have her half of the estate. Bill cut Clara out years ago. Bev decided to change it back, and she told Denise about it when they was having lunch."

"That sounds like Beverly. How'd Denise take the news?"

Earl squinted at the tile ceiling. "Well now, I hate to say it, but Denise wasn't a happy camper. She told Bev that was her decision, and she respected it, but her face got all red, and she had her fist clenched under the table." He demonstrated for me.

I smothered a grin. "Did Beverly say when she was going to see her lawyer?"

"She had an appointment for this coming Monday."

The decrease in inheritance gave Denise plenty of motive, because Beverly owned farm ground. The change would impact Jack too, if he managed to reconcile with Denise. However, Clara would've only benefited from killing her mother *after* the change to the will. Unless she didn't know her dad had cut her out.

Jack was average height, so he fit Clara's description of the shooter. Plus, he'd kept himself in shape and didn't have a belly like a lot of men his age. Denise was also a little taller than average.

"What're you thinking?" Earl asked.

"I don't know, so I'm glad it's not up to me to figure it out." I finished the last of my second cookie and glanced at my watch. "It was a pleasure talking with you, but I have to meet some friends. Thanks again."

"You're welcome. I reckon you'll find out who killed Beverly before long." He picked up the newspaper.

I hurried back to my truck, which was parked on Pearl Street. As I unlocked the door, my eyes fell on the United Methodist Church and the history museum next to it. It was easy to see how the mystery person had escaped Brandi's notice. The church completely obscured the driveway that led to the museum's parking lot.

I turned and looked across the street at Latte Conspiracies and Miller's Books, and one thought hammered me.

The new security cameras.

CHAPTER SEVEN

A fter texting Brandi and Ashley to walk the Wildcat Trail without me, I breezed in to Latte Conspiracies, got in line, and savored the smell of freshly brewed coffee. Hamlet and his sixteen-year-old brother Holden dashed around trying to keep up with the Saturday morning crowd.

Even though I'd already had coffee, I didn't feel right about plying information from Hamlet without buying a drink. I studied the menu and decided I could suffer through Bobbi Sue's newest creation—a Sasquatch Mocha. It was a white chocolate mocha with blackberry syrup.

Life was rough.

While I waited, I texted Brandi.

What time were you at the museum on Wednesday?

It took a few minutes, but she responded.

My mom sent a text right when I walked in. Time stamp says 4:13.

That was a huge help. I thanked her, dropped my phone into my purse, and stepped toward the counter.

Holden smiled. "Hey, *Georgia*."

There was no mistaking the increase in volume when he said my name. Hamlet looked up from the milk he was steaming and waved.

Clearly, I'd been talked about.

My face flamed. "Hey. I'll take a small Sasquatch Mocha." I held out my money and loyalty card.

"You got it."

Holden was shorter and stockier than his brother and played on the high school's tennis team. I was also fairly certain that he'd never be caught dead in a sweater vest since he was wearing a button-down shirt with a modern cut. While Holden made change, I glanced over my shoulder.

No one behind me waiting. Perfect timing.

"Hamlet will have your drink ready in a minute." Holden smirked and handed me my change and loyalty card.

"Thanks." I tucked them in my wallet.

Asking Hamlet for help might be a bad idea, but Bobbi Sue wouldn't be back before the wedding, so I didn't have a choice. I had to figure out who Beverly had argued with, and their security cameras were my best shot. Plus, I didn't want Cal wasting time running down a bunch of dead-end leads.

"A Sasquatch Mocha for Georgia Rae." Hamlet held out a large cup.

"But I only paid for—"

"I know. I upgraded you."

"Thank you. That's sweet." I'd be flying high from caffeine and sugar by the time I was finished. "Do you have a moment? I need your help with something related to Beverly's murder investigation."

I wasn't exactly a believer in superpowers, but Hamlet

demonstrated a remarkable level of speed and agility as he darted around the counter.

"At your service." He saluted. "Holden, I'm taking a break."

"All riiight."

Hamlet turned and glared at his squirrely brother. "To help Georgia with a *case*."

"Sure. Whatever." Holden's eyes gleamed.

Hamlet shook his head and faced me.

"I have stepbrothers like him," I said. "So I feel your pain."

He laughed. "How can I help?"

"Do your new security cameras have a view of Main Street?"

He tilted his head. "Yes. It won't be the clearest picture. Our camera is mounted on the back wall facing the door and windows, but you should be able to see cars and people passing by the shop—at least on this side of the street."

I glanced at the camera. "Could you show me footage from Wednesday starting at 4:13? I want to see who drove by shortly after that time."

"That's very precise."

I met his eyes. "I'm that good."

"I know." He winked.

Bad Georgia. Apparently, Nice Georgia had gone into hibernation for the winter. If she'd ever existed, in spite of my best efforts.

"Come on back."

I followed him down a narrow hall into Bobbi Sue's office. A shelf of alien figurines kept watch over the tidy desk with a picture of Bobbi Sue, Hemi, Hamlet, Holden, and the boys' sister Harper.

Hamlet sat and opened the laptop sitting on the desk. He rolled up his sleeves, revealing a tattoo of a cross made of nails.

I liked it. A lot.

Bad, bad, Georgia.

A few minutes later, he turned the computer toward me and showed me how to scroll through the footage. Then he stood and held out the chair. "Have a seat. I'll be right back after I check on Holden."

I set my coffee on the desk and zoomed in on the grainy footage, but that didn't help, so I zoomed out and focused on the cars passing by in a five-minute time frame starting at 4:13. The ceiling above the door and windows cut off the full view of the sidewalk across the street, but I recognized Brandi's coat, though I could only see her from the waist down when she entered the building. A few seconds later, she darted back out and disappeared in the alley between the museum and the church.

I reversed the footage and studied the passing cars. A cream-colored Cadillac. A mini-van. And a black Camry.

Just like Wanda's.

CHAPTER EIGHT

"Did you find what you need?" Hamlet leaned against the office's doorframe.

"Possibly." A lot of people drove black Camrys. Not to mention, I couldn't see the driver or distinguish the license plate. I searched more footage, hoping to see Jack's silver Chevy truck, the mysterious gray sedan, or even Denise's Escape with the nursing company logo, but nothing fitting those descriptions passed by.

"What are you looking for?" he asked.

I took a sip of my drink, which was a nice blend of sweetness and tartness. "One of my friends overheard Beverly arguing with someone at the history museum the day before she died, but we don't know who. I figured if I could find the person, we might get some insight into what was going on with Beverly."

"You're not buying the robbery-gone-wrong theory?"

"Not yet. My friend didn't get a look at the person in the room because he or she went out the back door. I thought I'd recognize a vehicle, but you know how busy Main Street is." I pointed to the Camry. "This car matches the description of someone Beverly might've been arguing with, but it could be anybody's, and I can't make out the plate." I unearthed my phone. "May I take a picture?"

"No problem."

"I appreciate it." I snapped and saved the picture.

Hamlet closed the laptop and stood. "Mom told me about how you solved Tara Fullerton's murder and figured out what happened to your church's youth pastor. Why get involved instead of letting law enforcement handle the cases?" He crossed his arms and studied me. "I'm not being critical. It's an honest question."

I gritted my teeth. "You mean why don't I let my *boyfriend* handle the investigations?" Was he suggesting there was trouble between Cal and me?

"I didn't say that." Hamlet's face remained expressionless.

He was either extremely unflappable or a masterful actor, which fed my annoyance. "You didn't have to." I put my hands on my hips. "For your information, Cal appreciates my help. And the people you mentioned—including Beverly—deserve justice."

"You think it's up to you to find it?" He sat on the edge of the desk.

"Someone has to," I snapped.

He flinched. "Is this about your dad? Because it has to be awful knowing his killer is—"

"Stop. I pay a therapist for this. I don't need your free psycho-analysis." I stomped toward the door but glanced back. "Thanks for your help."

I stormed out of Latte Conspiracies, but when I reached my truck, I'd taken enough deep breaths to calm down and consider my next steps.

I should run in to the museum to figure out who volunteered there on a regular basis, because it would make sense that a volunteer would use the back exit. Plus, I had the perfect idea about how to get the information I wanted.

After downing the rest of my Sasquatch Mocha, I entered the musty two-story brick building that housed the museum. A rack of brochures for local tourist attractions stood next to the door. A sign beckoned me to the permanent display and advertised a temporary exhibit showcasing the high school's former athletic stars.

Needing to focus on the task at hand, I fought a wave of sadness at the memory of walking through the museum with Daddy—one of the last things we'd done together before he'd been killed. With pride, he'd shown me the exhibit that'd commemorated the thirtieth anniversary of the state football championship.

The wood floor creaked as I strolled through the permanent exhibit looking at pictures, maps, and artifacts before making my way to the room that displayed photos, articles, trophies, and other memorabilia from teams and individuals whose accomplishments had brought honor to Wildcat Springs High School.

I stopped next to a black and white picture of the 1957 basketball team that'd won a sectional championship and picked out Grandpa Winston. Too bad Grandpa and Daddy hadn't passed any of their athletic ability to me—or my brother. My eyes fell on a skinny kid with ears that stuck out—Earl Smith had been the team's manager.

I continued through the exhibit, and more women appeared. I paused in front of a picture of Mallory Smith—better known to me now as Mallory Morris. She wore a basketball uniform and posed with the ball against her hip. She'd earned 1,167 career points during her time with the team and had received a college scholarship. She'd also had a successful stint coaching the girls' basketball team.

"If you have any questions, let me know."

I turned to face a cheery-faced, bald man who sported crimson IU suspenders and a name tag that read *Dwight*. A tuft of puffy white hair ringed his head above his ears.

"Thanks, Dwight. I'm ashamed to say I haven't been here in years."

He waved a hand. "Lots of people in town have never bothered to venture in, so don't beat yourself up."

"Thanks." I displayed my best smile. "I was wondering if you could help me with something." I stepped closer and lowered my voice. "My grandpa Ron Winston is marrying Wanda Morris next weekend."

"Are you Georgia?" His eyes lit up.

"Yes, sir."

"I've heard good things about you." He extended his hand and squared his shoulders. "Dwight Winters. It's an honor to meet our town's amateur sleuth. A real honor."

"Thank you." My face grew warm as I grasped his hand and we shook. "It's nice to meet you."

I remembered seeing his name on the football reunion program. He'd been on the planning committee with Daddy.

"How can I help?" Dwight asked.

"First, I need you to promise to keep quiet about what I'm going to ask," I whispered with way more drama than necessary.

"Absolutely." He drew his hand across his mouth as if he were zipping his lips.

"My aunt Rhonda and Wanda's daughter-in-law Mallory are throwing a bachelorette party later this week, and they asked me to make sure the ladies Wanda works with here are included." I flipped my braid over my shoulder and reassured myself that everything I was saying was true except the next part. "Do you have a list of people who volunteer here so we can double-check? Beverly was supposed to take care of that, but . . ." A lump formed in my throat.

"Such a shame about Beverly." Sadness flickered in his eyes. "I'd be happy to give you a list. In fact, I made a copy for that pretty new detective who works for the sheriff's department. Detective Hawk is her name, I think."

Pumping my fist behind my back, I widened my eyes and hoped it looked natural. "Do they suspect someone who worked *here*?"

"I don't know for sure. They probably want to talk to people Beverly spent time with, see if they observed anything strange. At least that's the gist of what Detective Hawk asked me." He lowered his voice. "I think some junkie was looking for drug money, and poor Beverly was an easy target living alone and all." He lumbered toward the office and motioned for me to follow. "Come on back, and I'll make that copy for you."

I trailed Dwight to the office and hovered in the doorway. A large table stood in the middle of the room, and it held a stack of yearbooks. Two large filing cabinets, a bookshelf laden with more yearbooks, and a desk with a computer, a scanner, and a phone stood against a wall. A microfiche reader sat next to the desk, and I was proud of myself for knowing what it was. A bulletin board hung next to the back door, and Dwight removed a calendar and took it to the copy machine in the opposite corner.

"It looks like you're busy with a project," I said.

"Sure are. The Wildcat Springs Memory Project to be exact. When no one's visiting, we've been scanning all the school's year-books into an online database. We enter the names of the folks on each page. Thataway people can search for their relatives and friends and the exact yearbook pages they're on pop up. It's been quite the undertaking, because we started with the three old township schools that were around before consolidation, and it's taken us a good ten years to make it to the 2010s." He turned from the copier and held out a paper. "Here you go."

"Thank you."

"That's all the volunteers and their phone numbers, though there aren't many of us. I'm about ready to start recruiting. Sure wish I could convince my buddy Earl Smith to help out again, but he lost interest a few years back. Not surprised though. Scanning yearbook pages isn't his cup of tea."

I took the list and tucked it into my purse. "Thanks. You've been a big help. I'll have to stop in again and look around when I have time."

"We'd be glad to have you." He studied me. "Your father, Ray, was a real nice guy. I had the pleasure of getting to know him years ago. We served on the state championship reunion committee together."

I moved across the creaky floor toward the exit. "He had a good time helping."

"I remember. Oh, the stories he and Jack Schultz told about their football days. They had us all in stitches." Dwight held up his index finger. "Come to think of it, I should ask Jack to help with a shift or two. I've heard he wants to retire from teaching soon."

I should split before I got drafted.

Behind me, the door opened, and a cool draft nipped my ankles. Two middle-aged women holding shopping bags from the antique mall down the street entered, and Dwight greeted them.

Perfect timing, ladies.

I waved the paper. "Thanks, again, Dwight. Have a good one."

When I got in my truck, I studied the paper. Dwight had given me a gold mine. Not only did it contain a list of volunteers, but it also had a work schedule for February. I was more than a little relieved to see Wanda hadn't worked on Wednesday.

But that didn't mean she hadn't stopped in for a visit.

Shaking off my unease, I looked at the other volunteers. Carol Powers, Roger Carlson, and Fiona Sylvan.

Roger wasn't scheduled for the entire month of February because he was a retired farmer who spent January through April in Fort Myers with his wife. Mrs. Powers had been my very strict junior English teacher, so I wasn't thrilled about knocking on her door and asking questions. I'd talk to Aunt Rhonda to make sure Mrs. Powers had been invited to the bachelorette party, so I could strike up a conversation with her and see what she knew.

Then there was Fiona. In light of this new information, and her affair with Jack Schultz, I needed to schedule a hair appointment with her—in person. Because, along with Beverly, Fiona had also been assigned to a shift at the museum last Wednesday.

"I was thinking an up-do because my dress for the wedding has a cutout in the back," I said to Fiona a few minutes after I'd left the museum and walked to the salon. I'd lucked out and caught her between appointments, and the place was quiet except for "Eternal Flame" blasting through the speakers. Even her receptionist was nowhere in sight.

"I agree." She adjusted her red-framed glasses that coordinated with a glittery American flag on her T-shirt. I'd heard she loved injectable fillers, and judging from the lack of wrinkles on her fifty-something face, I'd guess there was a lot more truth to that rumor than the one about me auditioning for *American Idol* six years ago.

I leaned against the reception desk. "The dress is dark blue lace, and I hope Cal loves it."

"I'm sure he will." Fiona glanced at the scissors clock on the wall, and I decided to take the hint and get to the point.

"Do you have any appointments for next Saturday? I know it's last minute, so if you don't, it's no big deal. I could always do a side braid."

"Let me check." Fiona opened her appointment book and ran her finger down the page. "I have a ten o'clock." She picked up a pencil with a large daisy on the end.

"That's perfect. I'm *so* excited about Grandpa marrying Wanda. She's such a sweet lady, and she knows how to deal with Grandpa—kind of like Grandma did." I twisted the amethyst ring that I'd inherited from her.

Fiona finished writing, looked up from her book, and closed it. "I'm happy for them both. Wanda's a nice person." She took a business card from the counter, wrote my appointment time on it, and handed it to me. "I'll see you Saturday."

I'd better act quick unless I wanted this little excursion to be a total failure. "I need some shampoo and conditioner." I pointed to the display case to my left and reached for bottles of shampoo and conditioner with a formula that allegedly tamed frizz.

Fiona totaled my purchase.

"You volunteer with Wanda at the museum, right?" I held out my debit card and tried not to cringe at the high price.

"Yeah. I'm a history nerd, so I take a few shifts every month."

"Did you happen to work with Beverly recently?" I had to confirm what I'd seen on the schedule, but I couldn't act like I knew too much.

Fiona nodded. "Wednesday we had a tour group from the retirement center in Richardville come through, so we always schedule two volunteers in case someone else comes in." She swiped my card. "That was the last time I saw Beverly."

"Did she seem upset about anything that day?" *Like your affair with her son-in-law?*

Fiona shook her head. "She wasn't her usual chatty self, but I didn't think much of it."

"Do you remember why?"

She pressed her lips together and returned my debit card. "We didn't have *time* to talk. I got there right before the group arrived, and I left as soon as they were done, because I had to cut and color Carol Powers's hair at three-thirty." She bagged the bottles and held out the sack.

I took my overpriced purchase. "Speaking of Beverly, I met Clara for the first time this week, and she told me you're friends. I bet it's been great to see her after all these years."

Fiona removed her glasses and set them on the counter. "With everything that happened, I feel *terrible* for encouraging her to come home and visit. I didn't want her to miss her chance to see Beverly again—like she did with her dad. But I never would've guessed . . ."

"Right."

She glanced at the clock again. "If you'll excuse me, I have some things to do before my next appointment, so I'll see you next Saturday." She stalked toward her back room.

I made a quick exit and headed to my truck. I needed to get home and do some farm bookkeeping before my double date that night, but when I passed Latte Conspiracies, my conscience throbbed like a finger that'd been whacked by a hammer.

Life Lesson #335: Don't zip around acting like you need a broom for transportation.

I owed Hamlet an apology for snapping at him. Taking a deep breath, I entered the shop. The morning crowd had dissipated, and only a few people were scattered at the tables. Holden stood behind the counter and grinned when I approached.

"Hamlet isn't here," he said.

I started to ask why he assumed I was looking for Hamlet but bit back my sharp retort when I remembered the broom. "Do you have his number, so I can text him?" I held out my phone.

Holden took it and typed with his thumbs. "I doubt you'll get an answer. He calls cell phones electronic leashes and only bought one to keep in his car because his ex-girlfriend made him." He handed my phone back.

He'd added the kiss-blowing emoji next to Hamlet's name.

"Really?"

He shrugged. "That's what you get for handing your phone to a sixteen-year-old."

I knew a pair of twenty-four-year-olds who weren't much better. "Thanks anyway. I'll catch Hamlet another time."

"He's working on his house. He definitely wouldn't mind if you stopped by."

No. He definitely wouldn't.

I parked next to a dumpster in Hamlet's driveway and stared at the run-down ranch. This place was more than a fixer upper. The poor house needed life support. Shutters had gone AWOL, and the paint-chipped blue ones that remained were crooked. A massive crack split the cement on the front porch. Overgrown box hedges looked like they were swallowing the house, and the white siding had dulled with dirt and yellowed with age.

I unbuckled my belt and told myself to tread carefully because the key to this visit was to apologize without giving him the idea that I was interested in anything more than a *very* casual friendship. When I got out, I heard thuds coming from inside the house.

It must be demo day.

I picked my way across the slushy snow on the driveway and entered the garage. I knocked on the back door, and when he didn't answer, I peeked into a shell of a kitchen that'd been taken down to the studs.

"Hamlet?" I went inside.

Toting a sledgehammer, he emerged from the back of the house and removed his respirator mask and safety goggles. Instead of a sweater vest, he sported a dusty Ball State hoodie. "Welcome to my disastrous abode." He surveyed me. "What brings you by?"

"Holden said I could find you here." I stepped inside and closed the door. "I'm sorry I snapped at you earlier. That was rude, and I don't know what got into me after you'd helped me and were so nice. You didn't deserve that, and I felt bad, and—"

"It's okay. I shouldn't have bugged you about investigating— but thanks for your apology." He put his sledgehammer on the floor. "I started the bathroom demo today. You missed the toilet removal."

I laughed. "Does that mean you would've recruited me if I'd been here a little earlier?"

"Yes. I would've considered it penance." His eyes twinkled. "Even now you're in danger of being put to work."

Time for a distraction move from the *Georgia Rae Winston Awkwardness Avoidance Handbook*. I pointed out the sliding glass door at the back yard. "Nice view."

The house backed up to a wooded area, and a concrete patio led to an empty in-ground pool.

"Thanks. As soon as the snow melts, I need to get rid of the pool. It'd be great to have one, but the concrete is a mess, and I don't have the funds to repair it."

I edged toward the door. "It looks like you have a lot of work to do, so I'll let you get busy."

He brushed bits of drywall from his sweatshirt. "I'm not sure what I was thinking, tackling such a big project, but I keep telling myself it'll all be worth the hassle when I'm done."

"Yeah." I glanced at the broken pieces of drywall littering the floor and thought of my small group's study of Ecclesiastes. *A time to tear down and a time to build.* "Things definitely have to get worse before they get better."

"My dad wants to meet you," Cal said that night while we were in his Jeep on our way to Bell's Dinner Theater in Richardville for our double date with Vanessa and her fiancé.

On the radio, Tim McGraw and Faith Hill were singing "The Rest of Our Life." Cal reached over and turned off the music.

A tiny flutter rippled through my stomach. Since Cal's immediate family was from Ohio, I'd never met any of them. His dad had recently moved to Florida after Cal's mother had divorced him. "Is he coming for Beverly's funeral?"

"Yes. Can you make it for dinner at my place on Monday night?"

"Sure." I ran my thumb over the seatbelt. "That'll be fun." Maybe if I said it out loud, I'd convince myself it was true.

Cal gave me a sideways glance, so apparently, I hadn't quite managed the necessary enthusiasm.

Bad Georgia.

Time for a new subject. "When I talked to Earl Smith this morning, he told me Beverly planned to revise her will to include Clara. Her husband cut Clara out years ago."

"Beverly told *Earl?*"

"No. He overheard Beverly telling Denise about it when they were eating lunch at Pizza Heaven. Denise wasn't very happy, which gives her a possible motive since Beverly owned a little over two-hundred acres of land that brings in a decent amount in cash rent every year. Or if her daughters wanted to sell, the land would bring a nice chunk of change at auction." I tried to read his expression to see if this information was new to him, but I couldn't tell. "Anyway, Grandpa and I farmed the land for Beverly, so that's how I know."

"I see." He kept his eyes on the road.

"Does Denise have an alibi for the night of Beverly's murder?"

Cal glanced in his rearview mirror. "No comment."

I should've known better than to try. "I've heard Denise's husband Jack is trying to reconcile with her after his affair with Fiona Sylvan. What if he killed Beverly before she could change her will so Denise would inherit all the money and land? He'd definitely benefit from that. Or what if he was after Clara, so she wouldn't tell Denise about his affair with Fiona? Or so Clara wouldn't be around to contest the will?"

"Those are some plausible theories." Cal kneaded the steering wheel. "Did you find out anything else from Earl?"

I stared out the car window into the darkness as we passed a house that still had Christmas lights lining the roof. I debated sharing my suspicions about Wanda. How would I explain how I'd gotten the information? I couldn't go there, since I didn't want to accuse my step-grandma-to-be.

"I talked to Fiona Sylvan at Sassy Salon because she volunteered with Wanda the day Brandi overheard the argument at the museum," I said.

"You think Beverly was telling Fiona to come clean about the affair?"

"I did. Until she told me she was cutting and coloring Carol Powers's hair starting at three-thirty."

"Did you follow up with Carol?"

"No, but I'll talk to her at Wanda's bachelorette party."

"Anything else?"

I wound a strand of hair around my finger. "Nope."

Through the years, Bell's Dinner Theater had been the venue for several of my birthday outings, girls' nights, and even an awkward blind date or two. The most notable dating incident had occurred with a guy my cousin J.T. set me up with about five years ago. After *South Pacific* was over, I was putting on my coat, and when I looked around, my date had vanished. Giving him the benefit of the doubt, I figured he needed the restroom, but when I made my way to the lobby, there he was by the door waiting and talking on the phone—with his ex-girlfriend.

Some enchanted evening *that* had turned out to be.

These memories washed over me as we entered the U-shaped theater and found our table on the right side of the second level. We'd have a great view of the stage that'd been designed to look like a giant juke box.

Vanessa stood and greeted us with a warm smile as Cal and I approached. She wore a creamy lace dress with a denim jacket, which complemented her auburn, shoulder-length hair. "I'm so glad you joined us. This is my fiancé, Curtis."

Curtis got up and extended a beefy hand. I tried not to cringe when he squeezed my hand as if he had something to prove. His mop of curly hair gave his face a boyish look, even though he had to be in his early thirties.

He slapped my shoulder and beamed. "Good to meet you." He turned to Cal and immediately started talking about the Pacers as I sat across from Vanessa.

"Thanks for inviting us." I glanced at the menu that'd been attached to the middle of a vinyl record.

"Oh, it's no trouble. Curtis doesn't love musicals, but he tolerates them for my sake. I think he's half hoping I'll find a fellow theater lover to see plays and musicals with, so he doesn't have to go all the time."

"Cal would probably say the same thing," I whispered.

She giggled. Our two men still hadn't taken a seat and were now busy talking about landscaping.

"How'd you and Curtis meet?" I ran my hand over the black-checkered tablecloth.

"My brother fixed us up." She flicked an adoring gaze at her fiancé. "Curtis runs a landscaping business, and my brother hired him in September to do some work at his house. When he found out Curtis was single, he asked if he'd be willing to meet me. He was, and the rest is history."

"You owe your brother extra-nice Christmas gifts for the rest of your life."

She laughed. "I know, right?"

"When are you getting married?"

"April." She opened her purse. "Want to see a picture of my dress? I bought it last weekend."

"Absolutely." They'd met in September. Cal and I had met in October. I told myself to knock off the comparisons —immediately.

She held out her phone, and I surveyed the mermaid style, strapless gown that looked great on her slim figure.

"I love it so much," she said.

"It's gorgeous." I took a drink of water. "You and Curtis had quite the whirlwind romance."

She blushed. "When you know, you know. We're both in our thirties, so there's no point in waiting around."

"Right." I forced a smile. I was thirty-one, and Cal was almost thirty-five.

A waitress in a poodle skirt came to my rescue and took our drink orders before inviting us to the buffet. As we walked to the stations that were arranged on the stage, I vowed to relax and enjoy the evening. Just because Vanessa and Curtis were on the fast track didn't mean that was right for Cal and me.

But was that what was really bothering me? Maybe it had more to do with Vanessa's other statement.

When you know, you know.

Did I know? Was I sure Cal was the man I wanted to marry? Did I need to be certain after a few months of dating? What if I was scared because this was my first serious relationship?

I took a plate from the table and pressed it to my chest as I waited in the pasta line.

I didn't have to decide right now. I just hoped I'd figure it out soon.

CHAPTER NINE

Sunday morning, I couldn't bring myself to go to Wildcat Springs Community Church. Knowing I wouldn't see Beverly making rounds talking to her friends between services knifed my heart. Not to mention Cal hadn't made my church his home and opted to attend the smaller Liberty Christian Church.

I'd attended a service with him once but didn't feel like being scrutinized by showing up again, so I drove into Richardville to Mom and Dan's church. Even though they were tired from their vacation, they made it, and after the service, we ate lunch at Salvador's Italian Restaurant while they gushed about how wonderful Hawaii had been.

I considered it a major victory that I only wanted to gag one time.

I surprised my mom when I asked to come back to their house after eating. They lived in a massive Tudor in Richardville's most exclusive subdivision. Dan retreated to their basement to watch college basketball and nap, while Mom and I made ourselves comfortable in the living room on opposite ends of her sofa.

"What have you got there?" Mom tucked her slim legs under

the skirt of her black shirt dress and motioned toward Beverly's manila envelope that I placed on the coffee table.

I picked it up. "Beverly gave me some photos before she died. There are quite a few of Dad."

Mom smoothed her honey-colored hair that she was growing out after a recent short haircut. Then, she withdrew the pictures and showed the one of Daddy and me in the combine cab. "We should've known then that you'd be the one who'd be the farmer."

I curled my feet under me and clutched a pillow to my chest. "Did Daddy ever mention the possibility of me joining him?"

Mom smiled ruefully. "No."

For some reason that was a kick in the gut.

"Ray was sure that Dakota would change his mind and want to farm." She shuffled through the stack of pictures. "Even though he tagged along with your daddy when he was little, Dakota resented the assumption that his future was already decided."

There'd been several arguments between Dakota and Daddy over that very subject. Daddy couldn't understand why Dakota wanted a career where he'd be cooped up in an office all day.

For a few minutes, Mom browsed the stack of pictures, and when she came upon the prom picture of Daddy and Clara, I knew it was now or never. "I met Clara Alspaugh earlier this week."

"She finally came home after all this time." Mom set the pictures on the coffee table.

I fingered the lace on the hem of my cobalt-colored sweater and filled Mom in on my initial encounter with Clara and her apology the next day. "Clara said her break-up with Daddy was her fault, but she let her family and friends think he was the reason she left."

Mom nodded. "That's true. It took a few years before Beverly and Bill were friendly to your daddy. Ray never knew exactly what happened that made Clara leave. He told me they had a big fight on prom night about an after-party she wanted to go to. He didn't think it was a good idea, because he'd heard there'd be drugs and alcohol. He took her home, and she went without him. The next day, Clara wouldn't talk to him, and after graduation a week later, she left. He always said he thought something bad had happened—like she'd been assaulted at the party—and he felt guilty for not going and protecting her. But he didn't have any proof, and she never made any accusations."

"When I talked to Wanda, she implied there was secret drama between Daddy and Clara that I should ask you about."

She scowled. "That ugly old rumor raises its head again," she muttered and shook her head. "The story was that Clara left town because she was pregnant, and your daddy didn't want to take responsibility for his child."

I drew a sharp breath.

Mom examined her French-tipped nails. "He assured me that wasn't even possible—and he was always a perfect gentleman with me. I never had any reason not to take him at his word, so if she *was* pregnant, it wasn't your dad's. But you know how some folks can be. Always wanting to think the worst about others." She crossed her arms. "It irritates me Wanda believes those rumors, or she would've set you straight right then instead of letting you stew about it. You'd think your grandpa would've told her the real story."

"How'd Daddy handle the rumors?"

"It bothered him, knowing people thought the worst of him. He told me it helped him learn to focus on what God thought of him and not to worry about what other people believed."

That sounded like Daddy.

"He always felt as if he'd somehow run Clara out of town, and we prayed for years that she'd return for Beverly and Bill's sake."

A lump formed in my throat. "He would've been thrilled to finally see the answer."

"You're right." She smiled sadly.

Later that night, I rolled into Wildcat Springs for Bible study at Ashley's place. I would've loved for Cal to join us, but I hadn't been able to convince him to come to our meetings. I respected his decision, but his reluctance bothered me more and more.

I parked and hurried across the street to her house. A few small mounds of melting snow remained on either side of Ashley's driveway.

Her front door was unlocked, so I went into the living room and came face-to-face with Hamlet. I froze and tried to keep the shock from my face. "Hey."

"Good evening, Georgia Rae. Evan invited me to join you all." Hamlet pointed to Evan Beckworth, who sat on a sofa engrossed in a discussion with Brandi. I'd had a crush on Evan for years—until Cal had come into my life.

"Welcome." I contorted my facial muscles into something I hoped passed for a smile. "I didn't know you and Evan were friends."

"I've been subbing at the high school to help fund my house flip, and we got acquainted at lunch."

"Well, I'm glad you could join us. Ashley's a great cook, so you're in for a good meal." I hoped my very polite and proper words sounded sincere as I turned my focus to Brandi and Evan's conversation.

"Dr. Burke had to back out, and since it's pretty much impossible to get a dentist to come in at the last minute, we'll have to go with another career instead . . ." Brandi glanced at me before exchanging a mischievous look with Evan, the school guidance counselor.

"What did I walk in on?" I looked back and forth between them.

"We couldn't convince you to give a presentation on farming for eighth-grade career day tomorrow, could we?" Brandi asked.

"There's a free lunch from Velda's Café." Evan winked. His handsome face and kind hazel eyes had been a major reason for my crush.

I took off my coat, tossed it on the chair with the others, and sat on the floor. "I love how you're bribing me with food." To Evan's credit, this was often a winning strategy with me.

"So you'll do it?" Brandi leaned forward. "It's a fifteen-minute segment, and you'll probably have a lot of questions."

I hitched my thumb toward Hamlet. "Why not have Hamlet talk about acting—or construction?"

He shook his head. "I've already committed to running the coffee shop tomorrow, or I'd be happy to step in."

"You'll be great, Georgia," Evan said.

I smothered a sigh. "Okay. I'll do it." I'd have to get over my phobia of middle school students.

J.T. sauntered in the front door, followed by engaged couple Heather and Dave.

When Ashley came out of the kitchen, she stared at J.T., and her cheeks tinged pink as she fluffed the bow on her cupcake-print apron. "The ziti and garlic bread are ready. I made chocolate silk and cherry crumb pies too."

"Sounds great!" J.T. said with more enthusiasm than I'd ever seen him muster. Well, except for when he was talking about tractors. He was a top salesman at Wildcat Springs Implement. He yanked off his Broncos sock cap, and everyone stared at him.

"Your man bun's gone." *Thank goodness.* He'd trimmed his honey-blond hair into a typical male haircut.

"It was time." He smoothed his hair and tossed the cap on the coat pile.

No kidding. Ashley had never commented positively or negatively about his long hair, but I wondered if she was the inspiration for his new do.

"It was freaking some of our older customers out, and there's no way I'm sacrificing my bottom line over my hair."

Well, there was my answer. So much for romantic motivation.

"It's getting cold, y'all." Ashley waved us into her kitchen.

"What's up with you and J.T.?" Brandi finished drying Ashley's baking dish and placed it on the marble counter after everyone else had left. "I've seen middle school kids with more game than the two of you."

I snorted as I tucked foil around the leftover cherry pie.

Norman, Ashley's tiger-striped cat that she'd rescued after Christmas, darted out of her bedroom. When people descended on Ashley's house, Norman's favorite hideout was underneath her bed, but he always made an appearance for Brandi and me. Norman stopped next to me, and I stooped to pet his head.

Ashley pulled her hands out of the soapy water and dried them on her apron. "I haven't answered him about going out."

"Why not?" Brandi put her hands on her hips.

"Don't you dare tell us it's because you're sad about him lopping off that man bun." I snickered. Out of habit, I slid the pie back from the counter's edge—though it wasn't necessary since Ashley didn't have a small horse of a dog that would gobble up whatever he could reach.

Ashley giggled. "He does look better, doesn't he?" She chewed her lip. "The timing's not right."

"Why not?" Brandi arched an eyebrow.

"Okay. I've been thinking about this for a long time." She untied her apron and tossed it on the counter. "I'm quitting my job and opening an art studio in Wildcat Springs."

I blinked at her. "What now?"

"Are you serious?" Brandi's normally mellow voice sounded downright squeaky.

"Of course, hon. I'm tired of engineering. It's not my passion. I never should've switched my major from art."

I had no idea she'd majored in art, although, the elaborate sketches she was always drawing on the chalkboard in my dining room should've given me a clue.

"Will your passion pay the bills?" Brandi-the-Practical asked.

"I have plenty of savings." She crossed her arms. "I've made good money the last six years."

"What'd your parents say?" Brandi folded the dishtowel and then picked up Ashley's apron and folded it too.

"I haven't told them."

"I see." Brandi set the apron on the counter and patted it.

I could tell the motherly part of her was having trouble holding back her opinions. "Well, what're they going to say?" I shrugged. "You're an adult."

"Exactly." Ashley lifted her chin.

"What's your vision for the studio?" I scooted out a bar stool and plopped down.

She clasped her hands. "All types of classes for adults and teens, and summer workshops for kids."

"Where will the classes be?" I asked.

"The building next to Pizza Heaven. It's a great location—right in the heart of town and across from the public parking lot."

"Should you start by teaching classes at night when most people can come anyway? Then when you get enough clients, you could quit your job?" Brandi knit her brows.

Brandi's suggestion—as usual—was full of wisdom, and I agreed with her conservative approach.

Ashley waved a hand. "Hon, I'll be fine." She put the baking dish in a cabinet and then faced us. "Enough about me." She motioned toward the living room. "Let's get comfy, because I'm dying to hear how things are going with Cal and Jon."

We moved to the living room, and Norman followed.

Brandi flopped on the couch as if she were a teenager. "Jon and I are done." She'd been dating the lawyer and triathlete for a couple of months after I'd suggested they meet. Going out with him had been her first major step back into the dating world.

"What? Why?" Now it was Ashley's turn to frown. She flipped a switch on her gas fireplace, and the flames flickered to life. When she returned to the couch, Norman hopped into her lap.

"No chemistry." Brandi crossed her arms. "Besides, if we're making excuses about why we can't date, I pick softball—practices start in a few weeks."

She coached the varsity team.

"You use that every year," I said. "You've got to come up with something more creative."

"If God wants me to have another husband, he'll bring someone." She flattened her lips and gave us her best teacher look.

"All right, hon. If you say so." Ashley stroked Norman's head and turned to me. "And you?"

"Things with Cal are going well."

His unwillingness to spend time with my friends loomed in my mind, and in our entire time of dating we'd never once talked about marriage. If Vanessa and Curtis were already engaged, then shouldn't Cal and I have at least *discussed* the possibility? Or was I expecting too much too soon and looking for trouble where it didn't exist?

"But . . . ?" Ashley studied me.

"Nothing. We enjoy each other's company." I picked a hang-nail. I did *not* want to be discussing this right now.

"Do you love him?" Brandi asked.

I bit off the hangnail. "Yes." The word came out with more confidence than I felt in that particular moment. "But we haven't told each other."

"Why not?" Ashley asked.

"I don't know." I scowled and fought the irritation rising in my chest. Why did I have to participate in this over-analysis of my relationship? "Remember how long it took Cal to kiss me? He likes to make sure things are right before he makes a move." I squirmed and pushed up my sweater sleeves. Why had she turned on that blasted fireplace?

"Good point," Ashley said. "I won't read anything into the lack of I *love yous*."

"Brian and I didn't tell each other 'I love you' until after we were engaged." Brandi's soothing tone should've comforted me, but it felt patronizing.

"Could you please turn off the fireplace? I'm dying over here." I fanned myself.

Brandi and Ashley exchanged glances.

"Sure, hon." Ashley set her cat on the couch, got up, and flipped the switch. When she sat back down, she picked up two fleece blankets from a basket by the couch and offered one to Brandi.

Brandi took the blanket and spread it over her legs. "Georgia, are you getting sick?" Concern flickered in her eyes.

"I'm not sick!" I shrieked. Tears stung my nose and eyes, and Norman shot off the couch and ran for cover. "I'm overwhelmed. Beverly was like a grandma to me. I could always go to her for advice and wisdom, and now she's gone, and we don't have any answers just like when Daddy died." A sob interrupted. "How much is one person supposed to take? None of this is fair! Do you think I wanted to lose my daddy when I was twenty-one? I still need him. I still need Beverly. How can God keep taking away people I love and letting their killers go free? He's supposed to care about justice. And don't you dare tell me I need to talk to my counselor because I've been there, done that, and it's not helping!"

I buried my face in my hands and sobbed.

Brandi and Ashley sandwiched me in a hug, and when I looked up, both of my friends had tears welling in their eyes.

"May I pray for you?" Brandi whispered.

I nodded.

"Lord, my heart aches for Georgia, and I believe yours does too. Please comfort my friend and her family. Beverly's family too. Bring the truth to light. Serve justice. God, please fix this." She took a deep breath. "Please work for good." Her voice broke.

"Lord, give Georgia wisdom in her relationship with Cal," Ashley said. "Help us to support her in whatever way she needs. Amen."

Everything in me wanted to believe God would come through and answer my friends' prayers, but my past experiences made it hard for me to trust. How long would I have to wait for answers?

If I were a betting woman, I'd have put money on forever.

CHAPTER TEN

"Do you have any more questions for Miss Winston?" Brandi asked the hundred or so eighth graders gathered in the school auditorium on Monday morning while I stood next to her and gripped the wooden podium.

Though Brandi had offered to let me off the hook after my meltdown the night before, I'd gone ahead and survived my career-day presentation. I showed two video clips that I'd taken while harvesting corn and soybeans last fall and talked about a typical day in the life of a farmer during each season. Now, it was almost time for me to retreat to the safety of my seat in the front row with the other guest speakers. I fidgeted with the guest ID badge hanging around my neck.

A skinny boy wearing a hoodie shot his hand in the air.

"Parker?"

"Miss Winston, will you go out with me? You can pick me up and take me to McDonald's. I'm low budget."

A few of the boys snickered and nudged him—one gave him a high-five—and a few of the girls gaped at him. One or two girls ducked their heads in shame by proxy.

My face burned. "I don't think—"

"Parker, that's not appropriate, and Miss Winston is spoken for." Brandi didn't flinch. "Let's give her a round of applause for sharing with us today."

How did she do this on a daily basis?

They obeyed, and there were even a few cheers. I hurried to my seat as the bell dinged and the students rushed out for lunch.

"Guests, please join us in the teacher workroom for sandwiches, salads, and desserts from Velda's," Brandi said. "Thanks again for being here today."

One of the other teachers led the way as we marched down the halls of Wildcat Springs Junior-Senior High School, and memories flooded back. The school even smelled the same. A mix of grease from the cafeteria, cleaning supplies, and the slightest hint of hog manure from the farm up the road. Brandi and I fell in behind the others as we passed the blue and gray lockers that'd been given a fresh coat of paint since my graduation.

"Did I do okay?"

"You were great. Even I learned a few things about farming." She studied me. "How are you doing today?"

"Better. Being here gave me something positive to focus on, so thank you."

"Glad I could help."

We passed the library entrance and rounded a corner into the senior hallway, where Hamlet and Mallory stood next to a water fountain.

"I thought he was running the coffee shop today," I muttered and ducked behind Brandi in hopes of taking the junior hallway to the teachers' lounge.

Mallory smiled and toasted her disposable coffee cup before turning and clicking across the terrazzo floor in her heels. Hamlet was making deliveries? Why?

He turned toward us before we could escape around the corner.

"Georgia Rae!" Hamlet raced toward us. "How was career day?" He wore a dark gray sweater vest.

"Brandi says I did fine."

He grinned. "I'm sure you were a hit with the boys."

"She was," Brandi said. "She even got—"

"Why aren't you at the coffee shop?" I blurted.

Hamlet didn't need to know I'd been fresh meat for ornery eighth grade boys.

He cleared his throat. "I . . . just . . . had to stop in to discuss an upcoming acting gig with Mrs. Morris." His cheeks turned pink, and he glanced back and forth between us before looking at the clock. "Your lunch time is waning, so I'll let you eat." He darted around us.

Weird.

"We'll see you around, Hamlet," Brandi called. "We'd love to have you come back to our Bible study group. I'm hosting a week from Sunday."

"That'd be wonderful. Good day, ladies." He waved but didn't slow his breakneck pace and nearly collided with a student turning the corner.

I bit back all my smart aleck comments begging for release. Instead, I followed Brandi into the teachers' lounge without a word. The room with a kitchenette, die cut machine, and a beat-up sofa was just like I remembered it from the few times I'd been sent there on errands for the teachers who'd trusted me. Like the rest of the school, it smelled as it always had—like stale coffee and mildew.

We filled our plates with sandwiches, chips, veggies, and sugar cookies, and since there was no room left at the tables, we took our food upstairs to Brandi's classroom.

On the cement-block wall above her desk, she'd painted a

quote from George Washington. "Perseverance and spirit have done wonders in all ages." At the side of the room, a large whiteboard held the week's agenda and assignments. Student desks held binders and iPads, and a few stray pencils littered the carpeted floor.

"With all the drama we were discussing last night, I forgot to tell you I followed the lead you gave me about Beverly." I crunched on a carrot.

Brandi rolled her eyes. "I never should've told you about that, and I shouldn't have suggested Beverly was talking to Wanda." She put her plate on her desk and motioned toward her chair. "Have a seat."

"Relax. I didn't put myself in any danger." I dropped into the comfy chair. "I asked Hamlet if I could look at the coffee shop's security camera footage that points out at the street."

"I'm sure he was happy to help." Brandi dragged an empty student desk next to hers, reached for a canister of wipes, and sanitized the desktop before grabbing her plate and her water mug from her desk.

The edge in her tone made me drop my turkey sandwich. "Wait. Do you have a thing for Hamlet? Is that why he was so flustered?"

She stared at me. "Not only is he eleven years younger than me, we're second cousins, remember?"

"Oh yeah." Bobbi Sue and Brandi's mom were first cousins. "I'd completely forgotten." I scanned my memory to recall if I'd put my foot in my mouth where Hamlet was concerned, and while I couldn't think of anything, I'd better watch it. So many people in this town being related to each other was another good reason not to talk badly about anyone—ever.

"It seems to me, a certain farmer is the reason Hamlet was flustered. If you weren't dating—"

"It'd still be a huge *no*. He's sweet, but if we got married and had kids, our poor offspring would be a twenty out of ten on the Social Awkwardness Meter."

She arched an eyebrow. "I see you've given it some thought."

I opened my mouth to protest, but a disturbing mental picture of a lanky, sweater-vest-clad young man sitting in a combine cab harvesting corn twenty-five years in the future side-tracked me. "Not really. Just a casual observation."

"If you say so." She spread her napkin in her lap. "What'd you and your new sidekick find on the coffee shop's security footage?"

"A car exactly like Wanda's passed by after you overheard Beverly yelling at the mystery person."

"She could've been driving by—or it could've been someone else's car."

"I know. And the mystery person isn't necessarily the killer." I fished a homemade potato chip out of the bag. "Fiona Sylvan was the only other volunteer scheduled to work that day, but she was allegedly back at her salon when the conversation happened." I popped the chip in my mouth.

"What else have you uncovered?"

"Jack Schultz had an affair with Fiona. What if Beverly found out and was trying to get him to come clean with Denise? I didn't see his truck on the security footage, but he could've left the museum through the Pearl Street exit."

"True." Brandi stabbed a forkful of pasta salad. "Jack's here today, you know."

"Why isn't he on bereavement leave?" Beverly's visitation was tonight, but maybe he'd been banned because of his problems with Denise.

"I wondered the same thing. He was supposed to pick up our food at Velda's during his prep time, so I went to his room to see if his sub would cover my class while I went out to get the food. But Jack was there and told me teaching is easier than dealing with family drama." Brandi wadded her sandwich wrapper. "He eats the next lunch. If you want to pretend you're getting another cookie, you could happen to run into him in the teachers' lounge in about ten minutes."

"Two things." I dragged a carrot through some ranch dip. "One. You confuse me. You simultaneously encourage and discourage my investigating."

She leaned back in the desk and crossed her arms. "Look, if Jack killed Beverly—and I'm not saying he did—I'd rather you talk to him here than tracking him down on your own—or at Beverly's funeral."

"Give me a little credit. I wouldn't bother him during a *funeral*." I huffed, though I had been known to ask questions *after* a funeral.

"Uh-huh. What's the second thing?"

"Everyone will definitely believe I'm coming back to the teachers' lounge for another cookie."

Before the bell rang, I left Brandi's classroom and headed to the teachers' lounge, barely beating the stampede of hyped-up middle school students returning from lunch.

Safely inside the empty room, I moseyed over to the kitchenette counter, picked up a napkin and an iced sugar cookie, and sat at the long table in the center of the room. A few seconds later, Jack, who also taught health in addition to coaching football, wandered in.

"Career day?" Jack asked as soon as he saw me.

"Yep. How's your family doing?"

Jack picked up two ham sandwiches. "Okay. I guess. I'm sure you've heard Denise and I are having trouble, but this whole tragedy is bringing us closer. Not looking forward to Beverly's visitation and funeral."

"There'll be a lot of people for sure. Why didn't you stay home and rest today?"

He sat across from me, and other teachers began filtering in, so he leaned closer and lowered his voice. "My football team didn't have a winning season, and you know how that goes. I need to toe the line if I want to keep my job."

Some people in our town took sports way too seriously and had no patience for a coach who had to rebuild a program with mediocre players. "Mrs. Morris wouldn't understand needing time off?"

His eyes darkened, and he glanced over his shoulder. "She's a workaholic, so she expects that out of the rest of us. Plus, I'm not one of her favorites." He unwrapped a ham sandwich and squeezed his fist around the paper.

"I'm sorry."

"It's the way it goes." He tossed the wrapper aside and took an such an aggressive bite that I actually felt sorry for the poor little sandwich.

I waited for him to swallow. "I have a quick question."

He furrowed his brow. "What's that?"

"I'm thinking about getting a gun and heard you might be able to help," I whispered.

"Sure." Jack released his culinary victim. "A lot of my female clients prefer a semi-automatic, but I sell a few revolvers to ladies now and then. That's what Denise prefers. Smith & Wesson .38 Special. Got one for her for Christmas a few years back." He shook his head. "But that's neither here nor there."

Denise owned a gun? My stomach flipped, but I tried not to react as I took the card. "Thank you."

He glanced toward the other teachers getting food. "Wanda

Morris brought in her first husband's collection for me to sell not long ago. There are some nice options that might work for you."

I forced a chuckle. "It'd be like keeping it in the family."

"Sure would. Anyway. Give me a call if you're interested. My business number's in the phone book." He took another vigorous bite.

"Will do." I crumpled my napkin. "One more thing. Do you know if Beverly was worried or upset about anything before she died?"

He chewed and then swallowed. "You're not on Team Interrupted Break-In, I see."

That was an odd way to put it. "No. Are you?"

"I don't know what to think." He ripped the extra lettuce off his second sandwich and tossed it aside. "Beverly was upset when she found out Fiona Sylvan and I had an affair. She saw a text message on Fiona's phone since they both volunteered at the museum."

"Did Beverly confront you?"

"Yeah. Even though Fiona and I are through, Beverly told me I needed to tell Denise before someone else did."

"When was this?"

"She stopped by the school to see me about two weeks ago." He held up a hand. "I know what you're thinking. That'd give me motive to silence Beverly. But I confessed to Denise right away. She kicked me out, and I've been living at an extended stay hotel in Richardville ever since." He popped the top off the water bottle and took a swig. "I've heard the rumors that since I sell guns part time, I look like a suspect, but I have a solid alibi. I was at B.J.'s Sports Bar in Richardville watching a Purdue basketball game with some buddies until Denise called and told me Beverly had been shot."

CHAPTER ELEVEN

After my conversation with Jack, I went home, ripped open a package of M&Ms, and stood in front of the blank chalk wall in my dining room. I had to make sense of everything I'd learned. I'd made a quick call to B.J.'s Sports Bar to confirm Jack's alibi, and the manager verified Jack had told me the truth. Now that Jack had been ruled out, I had to consider other people.

I shoved a few candies in my mouth.

With a piece of yellow chalk, I scrawled Denise's name along with the words *losing half of inheritance* and *access to a gun.* I didn't know if she had an alibi, but with Jack staying at a hotel, she'd probably been alone that night. And since her husband sold guns, she would've had access to them. It wouldn't have made sense for him to take the guns to a hotel.

I set aside the M&Ms and considered Wanda. While she might've been the mystery person at the museum, and she owned a gun, I'd yet to uncover a reasonable motive. However, she hadn't wanted to tell me what she'd been doing the night Beverly was killed. I didn't write *Wanda* on the board because I couldn't have Grandpa coming in here and seeing his fiancée's name.

I added Clara's name and put details about what I'd learned so far. *Secret reason for leaving Wildcat Springs. Friendship with Fiona Sylvan. Did she know about changes to her mother's will?*

Then there was Fiona. Though she and Clara had kept in touch, did Fiona know the real reason Clara had left town? Could Fiona have held a grudge against Beverly for helping put an end to her affair with Jack? Like Denise, she could've used her relationship with Jack to get easy access to a variety of guns. I'd have to see what I could find out at my hair appointment on Saturday morning.

I stared at the board and tried to piece everything together, but nothing was adding up. I tossed the chalk back in the basket and spent the afternoon cleaning my house—a task I didn't do often enough.

A few hours later, I paced in front of my closet, debating about what to wear for my dinner with Cal and his dad. Gus wandered in and dropped next to my bed with a moan.

"I hear you, boy."

A rock made itself at home in my gut every time I thought about our dinner plans. *Get a grip, Georgia Rae.* Cal had met my mom and stepdad. Now it was time for me to meet *his* family.

After trying on several outfits, I decided on a red tunic sweater that Cal had complimented me on a couple of weeks ago when we'd gone to a movie. I paired it with skinny jeans and boots.

After all, I needed to make a good impression on his dad.

Cal lived in an above-the-garage apartment that he rented from an elderly gentleman. When I'd first met him, he expressed interest in purchasing a small hobby farm in hopes of having a relaxing pastime. Now that we were dating, he'd stopped looking for a farm, and I interpreted that as a positive sign about the future of our relationship.

I took a deep breath as I climbed the wooden steps to Cal's apartment. Getting acquainted with his father would be a good test run for meeting his mom, which I dreaded ten times more.

In addition to the whole future-mother-in-law issue, I wasn't sure what kind of woman she was since she'd left Cal's dad for another man. The most I'd been able to learn about her from Cal was that she was a retired homicide detective who'd inspired his law enforcement career.

Cal's parents had divorced, and his dad, a former fire inspector, had moved from Cleveland to Florida where, according to Cal, he was playing the field in the retirement community where he'd purchased a house.

After Grandma Winston died, one of Grandpa's friends had tried to get him to retire and move to one of those neighborhoods. Grandpa refused, saying the whole concept of living with a bunch of other seniors freaked him out and that he'd be content to stay in Wildcat Springs with people of all ages.

"Hey." Cal said as he opened the door. He wore the camo-print apron I loved.

I stepped inside the apartment where butter, garlic, and warm air filled the compact space. While my kitchen was 1980s retro, Cal's took us back to the 1960s and 70s with the yellow floral wallpaper and brown appliances.

"Dinner smells great." I hugged him, and he gave me a quick peck on the cheek.

Cal's dad stepped forward with his hand extended. "Darrell Perkins."

When he smiled, I noticed Cal had inherited his dimple—but not much else—from his dad. Darrell was shorter than his son and had gray hair that he'd puffed up to try to disguise the thinning.

He'd clearly taken advantage of the Florida sun—or a spray tan booth.

I clasped his hand. "Georgia Winston. Nice to meet you."

"Go ahead and have a seat, and I'll dish everything up," Cal said.

Darrell chuckled. "Don't have to tell me twice. My son gets his cooking ability from his mother. I need directions on how to boil water."

"I'm not very adept in the kitchen myself." I sat across from Darrell at the dented table next to the door so I could make a quick exit, if necessary.

"My son tells me you're a farmer. How'd a pretty gal like you get into that?" He leaned back and crossed his arms.

Yikes.

"Family. My grandpa farms, and my dad did before he passed away. I was going to be a music teacher, but when Daddy died and Grandpa started talking about selling the farm, I stepped in. Most people don't think of girls taking over for their dads, but I love it."

"Money's better than teaching, right?"

I blinked.

"Don't answer that, Georgia." Cal set a plate filled with chicken, rice, and brussels sprouts in front of me. "Dad, are you kidding?"

"What? All you talked about the last two years in Cleveland was moving to the country and buying a hobby farm. It's awfully convenient you're taking up with a farmer." He cracked open a can of Diet Coke and poured it into a glass.

My appetite performed a vanishing act, and though I'd had Cal's brussels sprouts before and liked them, eating them now was going to take a major effort.

Eating *anything* would take effort.

Was my farm the only reason Cal was dating me? Not once

had that ever entered my mind, but apparently it should have since he lived in this outdated apartment.

How naïve was I? Is that what'd been bugging me lately? The sense that I was being used? I rearranged a few brussels sprouts.

Cal slapped Darrell's plate in front of him. "Why is it convenient, Dad?"

Did we need to hear Darrell say it out loud? His implication had been clear.

"Come on, son. You like nice things. You more than proved that during your time playing pro ball. Living large. Impressing women."

"Stop!" Cal's eyes blazed.

I gazed at his handsome face. Why wasn't Cal denying his dad's accusations?

Darrell raked his gaze over me. "Has he not told you about how he got used to all the dough? How he was a big spender? Why do you think he has to live in this old rat trap?" He emitted a chuckle that belonged to a villain in a cheesy movie. Was he seriously that bitter about his own life that he needed to come and ruin his son's?

No wonder Cal's mom had split.

I bit my tongue, so as not to dignify Darrell's questions with answers. I'd been farming for years and had never even seen myself as someone to be desired because of her profession—or land ownership. I'd always figured it was a turn-off since a lot of men around here had dreamed of being farmers when they were kids, and I was living their little-boy dreams.

Kerthud.

Cal's fist rested on the table. "That's enough!"

"Fine." Darrell spread his napkin in his lap and cut into his chicken as if nothing had happened.

"Let's pray first," Cal said.

"Go ahead." Darrell's fork and knife clattered against his plate.

When Cal was done blessing the food, I couldn't bring myself to meet his eyes as the silence grew.

I had to say something. Anything to get through this meal and to keep me from bolting out the door. "I'm sure Florida's nice in the winter. I know a lot of people around here who are snow-birds, and they love it. My mom's parents used to have a place in Fort Myers, but they've both passed away. My other grandpa's getting married on Saturday, and he and his fiancée Wanda are going to Disney World for their honeymoon. Isn't that the cutest thing? They're so excited. Well, as excited as my grandpa gets about that stuff. Wanda's been good for him, and she reminds me of my grandma because she brings out the fun side of him. You know my grandma was quite the talker. They say I get it from her, and I miss her because she had a wry sense of humor. Did you know any of my family from your visits to see your aunt Beverly?"

Darrell gaped at me as if it took him a minute to register that I'd paused to ask a question that required him to respond. He blinked. "No. I only visited a few times as a kid. Not much though because my grandparents died fairly young." He cut another piece of chicken. "Mom always thought Wildcat Springs was the best place on earth." There was no mistaking the edge in his voice. "Guess that rubbed off on her grandson."

"Well, I'm glad. Because your mom was right." I popped a sprout in my mouth, flashed Darrell a tight-lipped smile, and silently prayed God would get me through the meal.

"My dad can be a jerk." Cal shoved a skillet in the drawer under his stove and straightened up.

Can be a jerk? More like was a jerk.

"And I'm not dating you for your farm."

"I know." Fortunately, the words came out with more conviction than I felt, because how could I be sure?

"In spite of what my dad said, I have enough money to buy my own place. I'm waiting for the right one to come along."

"But you were a big spender?" Underneath the soapy water, I scrubbed the life out of a serving spoon before rinsing and handing it to Cal.

He swallowed. "I blew money on a fancy house and cars." He dried the spoon and tossed it in a drawer. "Dad makes it sound like I squandered everything, but I didn't. I have plenty saved for retirement—and that farm."

I nodded. "There were a lot of women?" I opened the drain and watched the suds swirl away.

"Yeah. When you play pro sports, women throw themselves at you."

I cringed and squeezed out the dishrag. "Not sure why I'd never thought about that."

"Because you don't know me as Cal-the-Baseball-Player." He opened a cabinet and put a stack of plates inside. "Look, I didn't take advantage of all the women because I was so focused on my career that I didn't want the distraction." He tossed the towel on the counter and wrapped his arms around me. "I thank God every day that I didn't." He lowered his head and kissed me as if he could make me forget the whole evening.

It almost worked.

CHAPTER TWELVE

T uesday morning, I woke up dreading the day's main event —attending Beverly's funeral. After dealing with Cal's dad the night before, I had no desire to encounter him again, so I waited until the last possible minute to slip into the back of the sanctuary at Wildcat Springs Community Church while the pianist played "How Great Thou Art."

Beverly's favorite hymn.

My throat thickened, so I distracted myself by studying the crowd. Cal and his dad sat near the front with Beverly's extended family. Grandpa and Wanda were a few rows in front of me. I'd never seen Earl Smith in a suit, but he'd donned one for the occasion and was sitting with his daughter Mallory and her husband, Tyler Morris.

The far sections on either side of the auditorium had been roped off, so people would fill the middle two sections of the church. Most of the people in the back were church members, and as I caught their eyes, we exchanged sad, half smiles of greeting.

A closed casket covered in a blanket of pink roses stood in

front of the steps leading to the stage, and at least ten floral arrangements flanked each side. The flowers' fragrance permeated the chilly air, and I wished I hadn't hung my coat on the rack in the foyer. My black jersey dress hadn't been the best choice for this icy day—though I had no plans to go to the cemetery.

The pianist finished playing, and Pastor Mark Williams rose and walked to the clear podium that stood in the middle of the stage.

"It's my joy and privilege to welcome you to this celebration of Beverly Alspaugh's life. Last year, when she was first diagnosed with cancer, Beverly made me promise her funeral would be a celebration of her homecoming in heaven." He paused and looked around the room. "We rejoice because Jesus Christ died for our sins—and our sister Beverly accepted Christ's gift to her. Now she's spending eternity with Jesus, free from pain and sorrow." He pressed his lips together, as if to collect himself.

Tears sprang into my eyes. My nose burned, and my tears spilled over.

"Please stand and sing with me the first hymn Beverly chose for this service."

As we rose, the pianist burst into the opening chords of "I'll Fly Away." I tried to sing, but I couldn't form the words.

When we were seated, the lights dimmed, and Beverly appeared in the video playing on the screen. I swiped my cheek with a tissue. Sitting in her favorite recliner, she wore her curly gray wig, and Miss Peacock cuddled on her lap. Recent pictures of Jack and Denise with their children and first grandchild were arranged on the end table next to her. Clara's high school senior picture stood next to them.

"Hello friends and family. If you're watching this, the Lord has decided to call me home." She stroked her dog's head. "I know this'll give some of you a start, but I don't care. The doctors say my prognosis is good, but the Lord has been after me to make this video in case they're wrong. The truth is, none of us knows how long we have, and cancer might not even be what takes me."

A soft murmur fluttered through the crowd. Had Beverly sensed she didn't have much time left?

"Thank you, Pastor Mark, for showing an old woman how to record this. I'm getting better with technology—even learning how to text with those emoji things. It's never too late to learn new skills."

I made a mental note to ask Pastor Mark when Beverly had made the recording.

"Every one of you listen carefully, and then you can get back to the funeral and say what you want about me—or maybe you won't have anything to say at all." She released a squirmy Miss Peacock. "Some of you don't know Jesus. You've been living to please yourself without a thought for where you're going to spend eternity. I know because I was once a rebel."

Beverly a rebel? That was hard to picture.

"I was sassy to my parents and was always doing what I wanted. One day, a traveling preacher came to town and held a tent revival. They were popular back when I was young and pretty."

A few people chuckled.

"That night, I went with my sister Dana to hear the preacher. When he was talking about sin, I knew he was speaking to me." She smiled. "God used that preacher's words to get my attention. Loved ones, Jesus died for your sins. Repent. Turn to him before it's too late, because I want to see you in heaven." She pointed at the camera.

The screen went black, and Pastor Mark continued with the funeral.

That afternoon while I was in my office analyzing our crop data from the previous year and ordering fertilizer for the upcoming season, Pastor Mark returned the call I'd made to him earlier.

"I see you're investigating again," he said.

I stood and stretched. "Just asking questions to help out my boyfriend. No big deal. I like to think one of my spiritual gifts is curiosity."

His laughter boomed, and I put my phone on speaker and set it on the desk.

"Nice try, but I don't think the Bible mentions that one." he said. "Now how can I help?"

"When did you help Beverly make that funeral video?"

"Let me check my calendar." The sound of flipping pages came through the line. "February eighth. She'd just bought a used smartphone and was getting accustomed to the change. After I took the video, I gave her some tips. She was most interested in the voice recording and note apps."

Weird. A week later, Beverly had been using her old phone when she got the call at the bridal shop. "Did she say why she upgraded? I thought she was happy with her old phone." I walked to the kitchen and opened a bag of cheese crackers. Gus followed along, so I tossed him one.

"My impression was that she wanted to learn something new. But she planned to stick with the old phone until she was comfortable using all the features on the smartphone."

"I see. Thanks for your help. So how are your grandkids?" He filled me in before we disconnected.

I nibbled a cracker, glad I'd followed my hunch. Perhaps I should take everything at face value. God led her to record her testimony, and she'd wanted to improve her technological skills.

My gut screamed otherwise.

CHAPTER THIRTEEN

Wednesday morning, I made good on my promise to Wanda that I'd help Grandpa finish packing and cleaning his house. Grandpa lived about three miles northwest of me, and as I drove the short distance, the cloudy skies made me long for spring. I turned into his driveway and wound through the woods, a wave of sadness rushing over me at the sight of the limestone house he and Grandma had built on the land he'd inherited from his father.

Grandma had wanted a new house, so in the 1970s, she and Grandpa had built her dream home.

Every so often, a memory of Grandma Winston would surface, and I'd find it hard to breathe. The same was true with Daddy, but today, remembering how Grandma used to pull pranks on the family—she had a plastic mouse that made appearances in the most inopportune places—caused my eyes to sting.

She'd been strong after losing her son, but she'd never fully recovered. I couldn't recall her pulling a prank during the last years of her life after Daddy's murder.

I parked next to a dumpster Grandpa had rented for purging

his life's belongings and ran around the side of the house. I entered through the kitchen door. "It's Georgia!"

"Come on in!" Grandpa shouted. "I'm upstairs heading to the attic!"

A few boxes sat on the dining room table, and all the family pictures had been removed from the paneled walls. I tromped up the floating stairs and found Grandpa in Aunt Rhonda's bedroom.

At seventy-seven, he was a heart attack survivor who fought to stay healthy and active. Today he sported a back brace over his denim shirt and jeans, and he had on his usual Rowe's Seeds cap to cover his bald head.

"You may be sorry you agreed to help." He opened the door to the walk-in attic, pulled on the string hanging from the ceiling, and when the bulb illuminated the space, I peered around him. A small pathway was lined on either side with boxes and old furniture stacked to the ceiling.

I closed my eyes. "Merciful heavens."

"Amen." He rested his hand on my shoulder. "You see anything you want, take it. I'm donating the furniture and anything else that's useful. Everything else is going in the dumpster."

I clapped my hands once and feigned perkiness. "Let's do this."

A couple of hours later, we had the attic's contents removed to the garage where we could sort everything. I claimed an antique dresser and a milk glass lamp for one of my guest rooms, and I sent pictures of end tables and headboards to Aunt Rhonda, Dakota, and my cousins Michelle and Eric to see if they wanted them.

While Grandpa went into town to get sandwiches from Pizza Heaven, I opened boxes to see if there was anything we needed to keep. Since Grandpa would have to be the decision maker for most of the contents, I moved quickly until I came to a box labeled *Ray's Room* in Grandma's neat cursive.

I missed seeing envelopes with *Georgia Rae* scrawled on the front in her handwriting.

I lifted the lid and sorted through the contents. There were some old comic books, cassette tapes, a couple of novels by Louis L'Amour—Westerns were Daddy's favorites—and an album with newspaper clippings from his high school football and baseball games. I added the album to my growing salvage pile and turned back to the box.

When I removed a copy of the novel, *Ride the Dark Trail*, an unopened envelope slipped out. I picked it up, turned it over, and examined it. Addressed to Daddy, the postmark was dated July 2, 1985, and Clara's name was on the return address.

I plopped on the concrete floor, rested my back against Grandpa's tool cabinet, and stared at the letter. Why had daddy never opened it? From the date, I guessed it was because he and Mom had been about to get married a couple of weeks later.

Even though I would've been curious if I had received such a letter, I had to admire him for putting it away and focusing on his upcoming wedding. I tapped the letter against my leg.

Should I open it or toss it in the dumpster? Truthfully, I wasn't even sure why I entertained the question. I'd known the minute it'd fallen out of the book that I planned to read it.

I carefully ripped it open and withdrew a piece of stationery with a daisy basket in the lower right-hand corner. Clara's loopy cursive was a tad sloppy, as if she'd hesitated about writing and wanted to finish before she could change her mind.

Dear Ray,

Congratulations on your upcoming marriage. I'm happy for you and Jill, and I've heard good things about her.

I'm writing to apologize for the way I left town after my

graduation. Even though you've moved on, I want you to know my leaving had nothing to do with you. I'm sorry I let my family think that, but at the time, blaming you was the easiest solution. I'm even more sorry your reputation suffered because of rumors about me being pregnant. You didn't deserve that.

If she'd felt bad, then why hadn't she come back and set the record straight? Besides, she'd been communicating with Fiona Sylvan. Couldn't she have let her know there was no truth to the story? Fiona cut the hair of half the women in town, so that rumor could've been shut down easily.

I wish I'd listened to you and never gone to that after-party on prom night. I did some drugs and got drunk. I went into the bedroom with a couple of different boys. Then I passed out and don't remember anything until the next morning except for hitting a deer on the way home. After that night, I was too ashamed to face you since you were right about the party being a mistake, and I figured you heard plenty of talk.

If Fiona had been there, that could be why she hadn't bothered to squash the rumors. She didn't want everyone knowing she'd been a part of a wild party, so she'd let Clara take the heat.

Please know that, in spite of the way things ended, I have happy memories of our time together. I wish you and Jill all the best.
    Sincerely,
    Clara

"Whatcha got there?" Grandpa stood next to me, holding a sack from Pizza Heaven.

I jumped. How had I not heard him come in the side door? Or smelled the sausage sandwiches. What kind of detective was I?

"This was in a box of daddy's things." I showed him the letter. "It was from Clara Alspaugh. I probably shouldn't have opened it, but with everything that's happened, I couldn't help myself."

"Don't blame you." He leaned closer to examine the letter. "I thought Nancy burned that blasted thing years ago. What's it say?" He patted his shirt pocket. "Don't know where I put my glasses."

I got up, and we went into the kitchen. I read the letter aloud while he found two tumblers from the nearly empty cabinets and filled them with water.

"Hmph. I told your grandma not to meddle and let Ray decide if he wanted to read it or not." He sat at the table. "The letter came right before your parents were about to get married, and your grandma was afraid Clara was trying to stir up trouble. I reckon she squirreled it away and forgot about it."

I joined him and set the letter aside. "Why would Grandma have assumed Clara was trying to stir up trouble?"

"Nancy never liked Clara." He removed our sandwiches from the bag and handed me one. "Thought she was trouble and would lead Ray down the wrong path. I didn't disagree, but I told her we needed to let Ray come to his own conclusion. That was hard for your grandma."

Clearly, difficulty minding one's own business was hereditary.

"Did you ever hear rumors about Clara—besides what everybody was saying about Daddy getting her pregnant?"

He squinted as if he were trying to remember. "That was a long time ago. I don't recall."

"Would it be okay if I sent a picture of the letter to Cal in case it can help him figure out Clara's past?"

"It's not going to bother me any. My son didn't do anything wrong." He unwrapped his sandwich.

I snapped the picture. The letter might not be significant, but if it was, Grandma's meddling might turn out to be a good thing after all.

———

"Thanks for the picture of that letter," Cal said later that afternoon. He'd called after I returned home from Grandpa's house to get ready for Wanda's bachelorette party.

"Do you think it could be important?" I picked up my blush brush from my bathroom counter and swiped my cheeks.

"We'll see. Vanessa and I are digging into Clara's background."

Sometimes I hated his non-answers. "Have you asked Clara about the letter?"

"We will."

Was it my imagination, or was there a hint of annoyance in his tone? Did he think I was trying to do his job for him when I was just trying to help? "Good."

Silence.

I ran my finger over my makeup brush. "I know it seems like I'm upset about the other night since I avoided you at the funeral, but I was just staying away from your dad, and—"

"I understand. We can talk later. I need to get back to work. Have fun at the party." He disconnected, and I stared at my phone on the counter and tried to ignore the swirl of uneasiness in my stomach.

I'd detected weariness in his voice, so he was probably tired because of his caseload at work.

Or was he tired of me?

CHAPTER FOURTEEN

Aunt Rhonda grabbed my arm and ushered me into Mallory Morris's spacious kitchen away from the crowd of women in her living room. A black and gold Sputnik chandelier shone on the finger foods displayed on the massive island. Chips, salsa, sandwiches, fruit, a veggie tray, and a slow cooker filled with meatballs, judging from the tangy smell.

"Am I going to get to meet your boyfriend on Saturday?" Aunt Rhonda whispered as if we were on a clandestine mission instead of at a bachelorette party.

It had originally been scheduled for the previous Saturday, but after news of Beverly's death, no one had been in a party mood. Even now it was a stretch, but Mallory had insisted on going ahead.

"Yes. Cal's coming with me." *As far as I know.*

Aunt Rhonda—from whom I'd inherited my height but not my curves—clasped her hands and squealed. "I can't wait. Do you think he's the one?" She looked me up and down with her piercing eyes as if she could detect the answer through telepathy.

"I hope so." I smiled. "We'll see."

"You'd make a beautiful June bride."

This June? How many times was I going to have variations of the same conversation? "There's no sense in rushing things."

"I wouldn't be so certain. I was done having kids by the time I was thirty-one. Those eggs of yours aren't getting any younger." She patted my abdomen.

I covered my tummy with both hands. *Jesus, please return for your church now because I'm ready for Heaven.* When no trumpet blast heralded the Lord's appearance, I cleared my throat. "I could always have my eggs harvested and frozen."

"That's never seemed like a good idea to me." Aunt Rhonda knit her brows. "Fresh is always best."

Aaannnddd there's Life Lesson # 2706, ladies and gentlemen.

I strolled to the opposite end of the island to inspect the desserts, and my mouth dropped. "What in the world?" I pointed to the twin pink mounds of cake with dark pink gumdrops in the middle of each.

Aunt Rhonda rolled her eyes as she ladled punch into a cup emblazoned with the words *Bride Tribe.* "I *told* Mallory to keep things classy, but she said since we weren't serving alcohol or hiring a stripper, we had to have something naughty."

"That's a little shocking for a dignified principal."

"Trust me." Aunt Rhonda took a sip of punch. "That woman has the sense of humor of a teenager. I guess that's what happens when you spend all that time in a high school." She chuckled and walked back into the living room.

I followed her toward the chatter. Mallory had decked out the room with pink streamers and silver balloons.

As I settled into a folding chair next to the couch, Wanda stood and clapped her hands. She wore a black sash with *Bride-to-be* written in gold script. A fuchsia feather boa adorned her neck, and a tiara nestled in her hair. "Thank you for coming tonight. As most of you know, I lost my dear friend last week."

She fished a tissue from her sweater sleeve. "Beverly was looking forward to celebrating my newfound happiness with Ron, and I wasn't sure we could go forward without her. But Mallory convinced me that she'd want me to have my party, so here we are." She dabbed her eyes. "I'll pray for our food, and then we can eat."

After the prayer, the hungriest women followed Wanda into the kitchen. Normally, I'd be in that crew, but I hung back and admired a painting of a chestnut-colored horse running through a field.

Carol Powers rested her hand on my arm. "Nice to see you again, Georgia."

"Hello, Mrs. Powers." I had a momentary flashback to junior English—and our grammar workbook. Oh, how Mrs. Powers adored grammar. My high school best friend Laura and I had called her Mrs. Grammar Guru behind her back, which in hindsight, she probably would've taken as a compliment.

"Are you okay? I know you thought highly of Beverly." Behind her glasses, her gray eyes filled with sympathy.

I nodded. "It's been a tough week for everyone."

"It's horrible. I taught with her for twenty years, and then we worked together at the museum. We were prepared that we might lose her to cancer, but . . ." She twisted the turquoise beads hanging around her neck and looked around the empty living room. "I'm not certain Beverly died because she interrupted a burglar," she whispered.

I did my best to look shocked even though I agreed. "Why?" No sense in leading her with my questions.

She tugged her denim jacket closed. "Beverly was very secretive about something before she died." She stepped closer. "And it wasn't because Clara was coming home after all these years."

"What was it?"

"I'm not sure, but last Thursday morning, I went to the

museum office to pick up my work schedule for March and found Beverly looking at microfiche. She didn't hear me come in, and she murmured something about 'prom night' into her phone."

"Her flip phone?"

"No, no. A smartphone. After a few seconds, I cleared my throat, and then she acted flustered when she realized I was there," Mrs. Powers said.

"What was she looking at?" *Way to end your sentence with a preposition, Georgia Rae.*

Mrs. Powers shook her head, apparently not noticing my error. "She turned off the power before I could see."

"What did she say?"

"Something like, 'Don't mind me.' She even took the film off the reader and concealed it under a pile of papers she was holding."

I rested my hand on Mrs. Powers's shoulder. "You should talk to Detective Perkins or Detective Hawk with the sheriff's department as soon as possible. What you witnessed could be important."

"I will." She nodded. "Thank you for listening."

"No problem. One more thing. Did you have a hair appointment with Fiona Sylvan at three-thirty last Wednesday?"

She patted her pixie cut. "I did. Why do you ask?"

"A source of mine overheard Beverly talking to someone at the museum on Wednesday afternoon, and I'm talking with everyone who volunteers there in case they know something, especially now that you're telling me Beverly was hiding something."

"Fiona and I are each other's alibis." She laughed and then elbowed me gently. "Now let's get some food before it's all gone." She headed for the kitchen.

Before I could make it out of the living room, the front door swung open, and Hamlet burst inside. A large box covered his torso, and it had a picture of bubbled paint and a scraper pushing the paint away, revealing bare wood underneath. The words *Take it Off* were printed in block text above the photo. A hat, made to look like a plastic cap, perched on his head.

He toted a portable speaker, flashed a broad grin, wiggled from side to side, and waved his wiry arm above his head.

"Hello, Georgia Rae."

Sweet baby chickens in a barnyard.

The edge of my mouth twitched, and I wanted to laugh but was afraid of encouraging him. "Ladies, the stripper's here!"

Hamlet strutted over to me. "Where's the guest of honor? I have a special dance prepared."

Was he wearing a sweater vest under that get-up?

I pointed to the entrance to the kitchen where a cluster of grandmas stood—filled plates in hand—gaping at Hamlet.

"Is this the acting job Mallory hired you for?" I asked.

He pressed his index finger over his lips. "A gentleman never reveals his secrets." He winked, set the speaker on the end table, and tapped his phone. Square dance music filled the room.

The ladies parted as Mallory guided Wanda to the front of the crowd while Hamlet did a routine that began with the Charleston, transitioned to the sprinkler, moved to a flurry of bell kicks, and ended with a lasso and horse-riding combo move. All while remaining in costume—except for the bottle-cap hat, which he plunked on Wanda's head.

"Whoo-hooo!" Wanda twirled her feather boa as I snapped a picture for posterity—though I'd never, ever be able to erase the mental picture for as long as I lived.

Later that night, I sat in Daddy's leather recliner with Gus at my feet while an episode of *Psych* played on DVD. I couldn't focus on Shawn and Gus's antics that usually made me laugh.

I'd left a message for Cal, telling him he needed to talk to Carol Powers about what she'd witnessed.

He hadn't called me back.

I shut off the TV and closed my eyes. Had Beverly uncovered a secret from her daughter's past that'd gotten her killed? I needed to talk to Clara again to see if she'd open up to me.

I threw aside the blanket covering my feet, found the packet of pictures Beverly had given me, and headed for my dining room. If Mrs. Powers was right about Beverly researching prom night, then I needed to take a closer look at the pictures.

I sat at the table and sorted through the photos, dividing them into categories. I grouped Daddy's football, prom, and his farming and family pictures.

The farming and family pictures were the most special and least helpful, so I set those aside along with the ones from his football days.

One by one, I looked at his pictures with Clara, paying close attention to the prom photos. I'd overlooked a couple of the group shots from prom night. One photo had been taken at Beverly's house, because I recognized the fireplace. Daddy and Clara were in the picture with Fiona Sylvan and a guy I didn't recognize, and Tyler and Mallory Morris.

I didn't know Clara had been friends with Tyler and Mallory.

There was another shot of all of them sitting at a table eating dinner, and I tacked it on my chalk wall along with the one of Daddy and Clara. They must've all gone together. That was a question for Clara, and if she didn't open up when I talked to her tomorrow, then I'd be sure to ask Fiona at my hair appointment.

CHAPTER FIFTEEN

D*ing dong.*

Gus rocketed toward my front door. I set my box of Cocoa Krispies on the kitchen counter and glanced at my robe and slippers. Then, my eyes fell on the microwave clock—8:01.

Too early in the morning for visitors.

I was up earlier than normal for the middle of winter because I'd promised to help Wanda decorate the church at ten. I smoothed my hair and swiped away the mascara smudges from under my eyes as I disarmed my security system and made my way to the front door with my favorite owl mug in hand. I hadn't slept much last night.

When I peeked through the sidelights, I saw my stepbrothers, Preston and Austin, standing on my porch.

What did the Twin Menaces want? I swung open the door. "Hey, guys! Come on in." I sounded about twenty times more welcoming than I felt.

Gus jostled past me and greeted them. Normally, I tried to prevent him from jumping on my guests, but I figured the boys deserved a little extra love for stopping by so early.

They exchanged concerned glances as they fended off my dog. Both were broad-shouldered former football players who'd been blessed with blond good looks. I'd had trouble telling them apart until Austin had let me in on the secret—he had a scar under his left eye from where he'd fallen on the fireplace corner as a kid.

"Look at her. She's obviously taking it hard." Preston pointed at me. "No makeup or anything.

Austin's mouth dropped open. "I've never seen her this way. Have you?"

"No, man." Preston gawked at me as if I were a circus sideshow.

I rolled my eyes. "Guys. It's the crack of dawn. Of course I'm not wearing makeup."

"Sissy, we're here for you." Austin rested a hand on my fuzzy robe.

"What are you talking about? I'm fine." Relatively speaking.

"Denial is never cool." Preston shook his head.

"Never good," Austin said. "Dude, we should've thought to bring her coffee from that joint she likes in town. That'd perk her up."

"I have some!" I pointed to my mug.

"I don't think it's working," Preston said.

"Will you tell me what's going on if I give you coffee?" I was proud of myself for not using the words pinging in my mind at that moment.

"Sure." Preston removed his coat.

Austin tossed his jacket on the bench. "We've got time before work."

I stomped toward my kitchen and wondered if all the recent progress I'd made with these idiots had somehow been obliterated. I filled squirrel and raccoon mugs and set them on the table in front of my stepbrothers. "Start talking."

Austin patted Traitor Gus's head. "We're going to need cream and sugar, sissy."

Not if I kill you first.

"Of course." I gave myself an A+ for how sweet I sounded as I yanked open the pantry door, retrieved a five-pound bag of sugar, and deposited it on the table with a thump.

"Most people put their sugar in a bowl." Preston's eyes gleamed.

"You're lucky I even have it." I put my hands on my hips. "Cal made spaghetti sauce a few weeks ago and complained when I didn't have any, so I bought a bag." I turned to the refrigerator. "But milk will have to do instead of cream." I yanked open the door, sniffed the milk, and plunked it on the table. "All good. Here you go."

"Thanks," they said in unison.

"Spoons, please." Austin tore into the sugar bag.

I produced the utensils for my needy stepsiblings. "Now will you please tell me what this visit is about?" I plopped down at the table.

They exchanged glances—again.

"I'm starting to think we got bad intel, Presty."

"You're right, Austy."

I buried my face in my hands and spoke through clenched teeth. "You can forget about being my sidekicks ever again if you don't tell me what's going on. Right. Now."

They stirred their coffee in tandem as if they'd choreographed the move.

"We thought you and Cal broke up," Preston finally said.

"What? Why?" I rubbed my temples.

They stirred some more.

"Because one of the other realtors in our office showed Cal a house in the country last night," Austin said.

What? My stomach took a nosedive. Had he been looking at

the house when I'd called? Had he made the appointment to look when he knew I'd be at the party?

Preston dumped sugar into his coffee. "And why would he do that when—?"

"Yeah. Yeah. I get it." I held up a hand. "Did he make an offer?"

"Not yet, but Cody thought he seemed interested," Austin said. "Do you want us to let you know if he does?"

"Yes." In a normal world that would be something Cal should tell me himself.

Concern filled Preston's expression. "I thought he was totally into you."

"Me too." I stood and poured myself more coffee.

"If he's jerking our sissy around, he'll have to answer to us," Austin said.

"That's right." Preston curled his fist.

For half a second, I almost felt sorry for Cal. "Thanks, guys. Let's not think the worst. He could be keeping his options open, or he wants to invest in a rental property." I cupped my hands around the mug and took a sip of coffee.

Or maybe, thanks to his dad, Cal now had something to prove.

After Preston and Austin left, I got in the shower, and when I stepped out, my phone was ringing.

"Hey, Wanda. Change of plans?" I asked as soon as I answered.

In the background, a high-pitched version of "Für Elise" played. She must've been at Pastry Delight. I set the phone on the bathroom counter and put it on speaker.

"No. But I'm sure you remember Beverly was supposed to

help us decorate. Said she had a vision for making the chapel into a winter wonderland. She spray-painted tree branches white and anchored them into buckets. She planned to string them with lights."

"Where are the trees?" I wrapped a towel around my hair and squeezed.

"I don't know," she said. "I hate to bug her family about them, but I think they're in her barn."

Good grief. Why didn't she ask instead of hinting? "I'll find them and bring them over."

"Thank you, Georgia. I don't know what I was thinking planning this ridiculous shindig."

"Now you sound like Grandpa." I laughed. "It'll be fun. The families will have a blast celebrating together, and it isn't like you're doing anything extravagant."

"Keep talking."

Most people didn't tell me that. "You look beautiful in your dress, and Grandpa will be blown away. Then there's your honeymoon, and the fact that you get to escape this deep freeze for your trip to Florida. You picked the best caterer in town, so the meal will be amazing. It'll be the wedding you always dreamed about."

"Thank you. Go find those trees. I'll have fresh muffins waiting when you get to the church."

"I'm on it." I disconnected and sent Facebook messages to Clara and Denise, hoping one of them would answer and give me the go-ahead to nose around their mother's barn. If I didn't get permission soon, I'd ask for forgiveness later.

I got ready, and when I still didn't have an answer from Beverly's daughters, I decided to wait a few more minutes. I lounged on my couch and called Ashley to leave a message, but to my surprise, she picked up.

"Did you quit your job already?" I straightened the magazines on my coffee table.

"Not yet." From her tone, I could tell she wanted to say more, but she must not have been able to.

I cringed. "I'm not on speaker, am I?" Sometimes she traveled with fellow coworkers, and if she'd answered while they were in the car with her, I might've blown her secret.

"No, but I'm walking into work now."

"Whew! So, I didn't call to ask about your employment status. Would you be willing to lend your artistic talents to Wanda and me after work? We're decorating the church and reception hall for the wedding and may need some help by then." I stood, walked to the window, and looked out at the pond in my backyard.

"Oh, hon. I'd love to, but I have plans tonight." She paused. "I decided to go out with J.T."

"Finally!" I pumped my fist in the air. "Where're you going?"

"To a movie. Coffee afterward. It's low key."

"Should I continue suppressing my squeal?"

"Yes. Channel that excitement into making Wanda's decorations beautiful, and if you need an opinion, shoot me some pictures, and I'll do my best to respond."

I walked into my kitchen. "That'd be great. I don't want our winter wedding wonderland to look like a winter wedding blunderland."

"You should never use puns." She giggled. "And definitely not when Hamlet's around, unless you want him to like you even more than he already does."

Heat crept into my face. "Noted." That was solid advice. "Have fun on your date with J.T. I want the scoop later."

We said our goodbyes, and I was emptying my dishwasher when I got a reply from Denise.

The trees are probably in the barn. If not, Clara should be at the house, or there's a key under the fake rock in the landscaping. Feel free to go in and search the basement if necessary. The police cleared the house and the crime scene cleaners have been there. Words I never thought I'd write.

I thanked Denise before I finished putting away my dishes and drove to Beverly's house.

I parked my truck next to the paint-chipped barn and hopped out. The brisk wind made me wonder if it was going to snow again, and the barren trees in Beverly's yard swayed.

I jogged to the house and knocked on the door. Miss Peacock barked, but a few minutes passed, and Clara didn't answer. I walked over to the garage and peered through the windows. Clara's red hatchback was parked next to Beverly's car.

Maybe Clara was asleep or in the shower. I checked my messages to see if she'd answered, but she hadn't.

If her car hadn't been in the garage, I would've used the key to go in and look for Beverly's smartphone. Instead, I hurried to the barn, unhooked the latch, heaved the door aside, and surveyed the contents. To my left was a riding lawn mower, and I caught a faint whiff of gasoline.

The cats that once lived in this barn had been given new homes, since Miss Peacock had kept Beverly busy. To my right, in the back corner, stood the grove of spray-painted trees. "Cool." We'd be able to make the church look pretty.

I headed over and inspected the large plastic tub sitting next to the trees. It contained boxes of white string lights as well as silver fabric Beverly must have intended to use to disguise the five-gallon buckets that anchored the branches. I hoped the material hadn't absorbed the barn's mustiness.

Swish. Thud. Click.

I froze. The barn darkened, and a bit of light streamed in

through the windows at the top. Goosebumps rose on my arms. There's no way that heavy door would've closed on its own—even with the wind.

"Clara?"

I dropped the tree and raced to the door. Pulling on it, I prayed it would budge, but the door held fast. "Help! Clara!" I slapped my palm against the door and fought back a slew of naughty words when I realized my phone was in my truck. Who knew how long it would be before Wanda figured out something was wrong? Gravel crunched as a vehicle exited the driveway and zoomed down the road.

I slumped against the rough wall, and my pulse pounded against my neck. A gust of wind howled. I rubbed my arms and caught a whiff of smoke filtering in through the cracks.

"No, no, no!"

Flames skirted along the foundation.

"Are you *kidding* me?"

Yanking my scarf over my nose and mouth, I took in my surroundings. "Lord, help me find a way out."

The narrow windows at the top were too high for me to reach, and even if I could scale the walls, they weren't wide enough for me to pass through—and my curves weren't to blame. Even petite Ashley wouldn't be able to wiggle through those windows.

I raced the perimeter, pressing the walls in search of a gap or a weakness. The wood on the back wall crackled. When I approached the corner behind the lawn mower, my heart kerplopped to my feet.

Clara sprawled face down in the dirt.

CHAPTER SIXTEEN

Kneeling beside Clara, I pressed my fingers to her neck, praying for a pulse.

Nothing.

Blood pooled under the side of her head.

There was a chance her pulse was so faint I couldn't detect it, and there was no way I'd leave her behind. But I had to find a way out first.

The smoke thickened, and the heat taunted me.

I returned to the door. Instead of giving it another pull, I bent and examined the vertical boards, rotting along the bottom. One slat was loose, and bracing myself, I snapped it off.

I glanced over my shoulder. The fire flickered up the back wall behind the trees. It wouldn't be long before the barn caved in.

Grasping a second board, I tugged it and fell backward onto my bottom. I shot up and tried again. This time the board loosened, and I yanked it hard. The wood splintered and cracked. I bent next to the hole, pulled down my scarf, and gulped fresh air.

Please, God. Help us get out.

I covered my nose and mouth again before ripping off a third and fourth board, tearing the flesh on my palms. The fire edged closer. I dove through the opening, wiggling my hips through the ragged hole to snake my way to freedom.

Clawing my way up the door for support, I unhooked the latch and heaved the door open. Flames licked closer, and I crawled across the dirt to Clara. I looped my arms underneath hers, and, holding my breath, I stood and dragged her through the door.

I coughed and heaved her across the gravel driveway until I reached the brown grass and crumpled onto my backside. Sirens wailed, and I took another deep breath.

My truck was too close to the barn. I had to move it before the firetrucks arrived. Crawling away from Clara, I sucked in another breath. Only a few more feet.

I grasped the door handle, leaving a blood smear. I could do it. I had to move the truck. Cranking the engine, I lolled against the seat, threw the truck in drive and steered it into the grass, far from the driveway.

The barn walls buckled, and the roof collapsed into the flames.

"Is Clara alive?" I asked in my hoarse voice as soon as Cal walked into my room in the Richard County ER that afternoon. At my insistence, Mom and Dan had gone to the cafeteria to get some lunch. Mom had been in tears when they'd arrived, and it'd taken Dan and me the better part of an hour to reassure her that I'd be fine.

"Are you okay?" Concern and fear mingled in his expression as he slid off his coat.

"I've been feeling better since I've been lying here sucking in oxygen." I pointed to the nasal canula. "The doctor ordered a bunch of tests and said I'm lucky. I only have mild smoke inhalation." I lifted my bandaged hands. "And a few cuts. I'll get to bust out of here later."

He kissed my forehead before pulling a chair over to the bed. "You're not going home alone."

"Are you volunteering to sleep in my guest room?" Though I wouldn't mind, I wasn't sure how that'd look to my family and friends.

He dimpled and met my gaze. "I think we should avoid that situation."

"Right." I shifted as my face hit its boiling point. "Mom will insist I stay with her and Dan anyway," I muttered.

"Good. Now what were you doing in Aunt Beverly's barn?"

"You never answered my question about Clara." I tilted the bed up.

He ran his fingers through his hair. "She passed away."

Tears stung my eyes. "No. Maybe if I'd have gotten her out more quickly—"

"It's not your fault. I'm guessing the autopsy will confirm she died from the blow to her head. She was probably already gone when you dragged her out." He grasped my other hand. "I still don't understand why you were in Aunt Beverly's barn."

"Beverly made decorative trees for the wedding, and I was there to pick them up because Wanda asked me to find them. We all figured they were probably in the barn." I twisted a wad of blanket. "I even sent Facebook messages to Clara and Denise to ask permission. Denise told me to go ahead and that Clara was there. I went to the house first because I wanted to talk to Clara, but when she didn't answer the door, I went out to the barn." I sat up straighter and rested my hand on his bicep. "Where's Miss Peacock?"

"At Beverly's house. I'll make sure someone takes care of her. Even if I have to do it myself."

That was sweet of him.

Cal brushed a strand of my smoky hair off my face. "Tell me what happened next."

"I was looking at the trees when someone locked the door and set the barn on fire. I didn't see Clara until I was looking for a way out, because she was unconscious in the corner behind the lawn mower."

"Who else knew you were going to Aunt Beverly's besides Denise and Wanda?"

"I don't know. Wanda was at Pastry Delight when she called, so anyone could've overheard her hinting for me to get the trees from Beverly's barn."

Wanda had bought the muffins at a little after nine that morning, and the shop had a regular customer every day at that time.

"What're you thinking?" Cal asked.

I chewed my lip. Surely Old Man Smith didn't have anything to do with the murders. Showing up at Beverly's the night she'd been shot only had to do with his general nosiness, right? But Cal had already questioned how reliable Earl was, and we had to consider every angle.

"Earl Smith goes to Pastry Delight every day between nine and ten. He could've overheard Wanda talking to me and decided to take Clara and me out. He could've parked and waited behind Beverly's old stables because I definitely didn't hear a vehicle pull into the driveway."

"Okay. Maybe. But what about a motive?" Cal scrubbed his hand over his face. "Why would Earl murder Beverly and Clara —and try to kill you?"

"I don't know." I stared at my hands and tried to make sense of everything. "Did you get my message last night? About what

Carol Powers witnessed with the smartphone and the microfiche reader?"

"Yes."

I didn't even want to ask why he hadn't called me back. "*Was* there a smartphone at Beverly's house?"

"Not that I'm aware of, but I'll double check."

"Maybe Beverly figured out a secret about Clara's past, and somebody felt threatened and silenced them both. Or Denise killed her mom and her sister because of the will and then decided to take me out because I've been asking questions."

"You focus on recovering. I've got this." He bent over and gave me a gentle kiss on the lips. "I'll talk to Earl and dig into Wanda's background—just in case." He walked toward the door.

"Wait."

Cal turned around.

"Is it true you looked at a house in the country last night?"

"How did . . . ?" He furrowed his brow and then closed his eyes. "Preston and Austin."

"Were you going to tell me?" I didn't manage to keep the tremor out of my voice.

"I've been working with a realtor since I moved here, and when this place came on the market, he sent me the listing because it's what I've been looking for."

"Did you put in an offer?"

"Not yet." He shoved his hands in his leather jacket pockets.

"But you're going to?"

"Maybe. I haven't decided." His phone buzzed, and he took it out and glanced at it. "I need to go. We'll discuss this later." He strode out the door.

I wasn't looking forward to that conversation.

"Mom, I promise. I'm fine," I croaked as I shifted to adjust my position on her basement couch that evening after the ER doctor had released me. I hadn't put up a fight when Mom insisted on me staying in her guest room as I'd predicted. She'd even invited Cal for dinner and to stay the night in Preston's old bedroom, and he'd agreed.

Gus rested on the floor next to me, even though I was certain Dan had never before allowed an animal in his fancy house.

Mom draped a blanket over my feet. "I need to make you some tea with honey for your voice." She patted my shoulder and handed me an issue of *Good Housekeeping*. "I'll go do that."

"Thank you." I had to be able to sing at the wedding on Saturday.

Mom hurried upstairs to the kitchen where she'd put herb-crusted chicken in the oven. The scent of garlic, butter, and oregano made its way to the basement. A random thought assailed me. Would Cal like me better if I cooked?

I shoved the thought away and busied myself by flipping pages, which didn't distract me as much as I'd hoped. I put the magazine aside as Mom returned with a mug of tea, which she handed me before sitting at my feet.

I tested the tea with the edge of my lip, but it was too hot to drink. "Beverly and Clara's murders have me thinking a lot about Daddy's murder."

Mom folded her hands. "I know. Ever since that night, I've gone over and over his last days in my head trying to remember something—anything—that could help the detectives break the case."

"Me too. It's hard to accept that his death was random." Tears filled my eyes. "But having answers doesn't change the outcome—for Daddy or Beverly."

"Or Clara."

"Do you think God has forgotten us?" I whispered. "It feels that way. Like justice doesn't matter to him."

"Oh, sweetie, I know. Trust me." She slid off the couch and knelt beside me. "Just because we feel a certain way about God doesn't make it true. I can't tell you how many times after your dad died I sat with my Bible open searching for reminders about God's true character. I was so angry at God for taking my husband—and my children's dad. But every time I got my mind off my feelings and focused on who God is, my perspective changed." She kissed my forehead. "I know it's not easy, but that's what helped me."

I nodded. *God, please help my perspective.*

CHAPTER SEVENTEEN

Thursday night, Cal had arrived at Mom and Dan's house for a late dinner, and there hadn't been an opportunity to discuss his house situation. The next morning, he needed to talk to Taryn Anderson at Pastry Delight and invited me to go with him before I had to help Grandpa and Wanda decorate.

I drove into town, and he followed behind. When we walked into the bakery, we were the only customers.

"What can I get for you this morning?" Taryn directed a flirty smile—as sickeningly sweet as her shop's pink walls—at Cal.

I clenched my jaw and approached the counter. "Two chocolate chip cookies, please." My voice was still hoarse from the smoke.

"How about you?" Taryn raked her gaze over my boyfriend.

"Nothing for me, thanks." He took out his wallet and handed her a few bills.

"Thank you," I said.

"You're welcome." He smiled at me before turning to Taryn. "Do you remember if Earl Smith was in here yesterday at his regular time?"

Taryn nodded, and her top knot bounced as she handed him his change. "He bought his usual three cookies at a little after nine and then left a little before ten."

Plenty of time to kill Clara and set the fire.

"So it was a regular day for him." Cal handed me the cookies.

Taryn glanced at me. "Not exactly."

Cal's forehead wrinkled. "What was different?"

She ran her hand over her spotless counter. "I shouldn't say."

"Not even if it could help a murder investigation? If you know something, I need you to tell me," he said.

She fiddled with the strap on her white apron. "Wanda Morris came in, and she was on the phone. Something about trees in a barn."

"Wedding decorations," I said.

"Gotcha. Anyway, after she finished her conversation, we confirmed her wedding cake order, and she bought half a dozen double chocolate muffins. She seemed like she was in a hurry, but when I was done waiting on her, she sat at Earl's table, gave him an envelope, and they talked."

"Did you happen to overhear what they were discussing?" Cal asked.

"Most of it. That's the problem." She flicked her gaze in my direction.

I should probably volunteer to leave, but my boyfriend had invited me, and I was going to glean every possible tidbit until I was told to scram. "Don't mind me. It could be important."

She glanced toward the pastry case. "I couldn't hear the first part of their conversation because I was refilling cookie trays in the back, but when I came out, Earl told Wanda not to marry Ron Winston."

My jaw dropped. *Seriously?*

"I'm sorry," she said quickly. "I don't want to cause trouble. I'm just reporting what I heard."

"It's fine." Cal gave her a smile that was ten times more reassuring than necessary. "Did Earl elaborate?"

"He said Ron was abusive to his first wife, and he didn't want to see Wanda get into the same mess."

"That's not true!" I croaked. My fingers curled into a fist. "He's making that up. My grandparents didn't have a perfect marriage, but Grandpa never hurt Grandma. She wouldn't have tolerated abuse."

Taryn raised both hands. "I'm sorry."

"How did Wanda react?" Cal asked.

"Like Georgia did. She denied it, but Earl told her Ron wasn't who he appeared to be and that he knew things about Ron's past."

"What things?" I managed to choke out.

"Wanda asked him the same question, but when he didn't go into detail, she stormed out."

"How did Earl act around Wanda *before* this conversation?" Cal asked.

Taryn studied him. "Like a kid with a crush. He perked up when she came in. Flirted with her a little, even though he knew she was taken." She smirked at me. "Basically, Earl acted the same way everybody says Hamlet Miller acts around Georgia."

Cal's eyes clouded as he looked my way.

That did it. I would never, ever darken the door of Pastry Delight again. One catty baker was enough to turn me off cookies for life.

"Is there anything else?" Cal asked.

"No. I'm sorry. I can call if I remember something." She looked at him with a little too much hopefulness in her expression.

Seriously? I'm right here.

"Thanks for your time," he said.

We left the bakery and walked down the sidewalk in silence.

Town was starting to awaken as shops and stores opened. When we came to my truck, I opened the door and tossed my purse inside. "Are we going to talk about what Taryn said?"

"If you want."

I slammed the door. "First of all, Earl's lying about my grandpa."

"Given Earl's reputation, I tend to agree."

It wasn't lost on me that he was hedging, but I'd deal with that later. "And I can't help how Hamlet acts."

"I know. But when were you going to tell me he's been coming to your Bible study?"

I bristled. He was *not* going to blame that on me. "When were you going to come and find out for yourself?" I put my hands on my hips and stared at him. "By the way how *did* you know?"

"I drove by and saw him leaving Ashley's house last Sunday." Cal's expression remained unchanged, and he ran his fingers through his hair. "Forget about him. I got a call on the way here, and I have some news."

"What's that?" *Sure. Ignore my other question.*

"Yesterday afternoon I put in an offer on the house, and the seller accepted."

My stomach lurched. "Congratulations. I'd like to see it sometime." I wasn't quite sure how I was forming words that made any sense.

He removed his phone from his pocket and held it out so I could see. "Here's the listing. The pictures don't do it justice, but I love the original staircase and woodwork." He scrolled through the pictures.

The house was beautiful and didn't need a single update because the sellers had clearly done work within the last few years, judging from the modern farmhouse décor that was so prevalent. "How much land?"

"Two acres. Has some established trees."

I wrapped my arms around my waist. "That's great. Give J.T. a call if you need a lawnmower."

"Absolutely."

A burgundy minivan parked behind my truck, and a tall, middle-aged man wearing a tweed flat cap got out. Cal nodded at him as he approached.

"Howdy, Perkins. This Georgia?" His weathered face crinkled into a smile.

"Sure is." Cal turned to me. "Georgia, this is my buddy Pat Hillyer. He's a retired cop who owes me a favor, so he's going to keep an eye on you today." His tone made it clear he wouldn't take *no* for an answer.

I wanted to protest that I didn't need a babysitter, but since I liked living, I literally bit my tongue as I looked back and forth between the men. "How's this going to work?"

"I'll keep my distance. You'll hardly know I'm around," Pat said. "I've been working in private security for five years." He fished a piece of gum from his bomber jacket pocket and popped it in his mouth.

Cal leaned over and gave me a quick peck on the lips. "I have to get back to work, but I'll see you tonight at the rehearsal. Be good for Pat."

As I watched him stride down the street, I opted to look on the bright side. At least Cal had cared enough about me to provide a bodyguard.

Thursday night, Grandpa and some of their friends had replaced the trees lost in the fire, but someone had to purchase new white string lights. Wanda had assigned that task to me, and after leaving Pastry Delight, I drove to William's Home

Supply in Richardville to complete my mission with Pat hot on my tail.

In the store, I filled my cart with every box of white lights in stock while Pat observed from a distance. I was high-tailing it to the checkout when Hamlet darted out of the aisle that held toilets and vanities.

I swerved to miss him, and he jumped out of my path.

"I'm so sorry," I said.

"No problem." Red crept up his neck. "Are you okay? I heard about the fire, and I almost called you, but I didn't want to overstep."

"I'm fine." Except for my hoarse voice and sore hands.

"It's hard for me to fathom why anyone would want to hurt you." He shifted. "Is your boyfriend taking care of you?"

"Yes." I pressed my lips together and gave a reassuring nod to Pat who'd edged closer. Would he report this encounter to Cal?

"Are you sure?" Concern radiated from Hamlet's eyes.

"I'd better be on my way to the checkout. We have a lot more decorating to do for the wedding." I pointed to my cart full of lights. "Yesterday's fiasco put us behind." I set my jaw, turned toward the front of the store, and blazed toward the checkout with my rattling cart, praying Hamlet wouldn't notice Pat following me and start asking a bunch of questions.

"I'll walk with you." He caught up to me. "I'm pricing pieces for my bathrooms."

I passed by the paint samples and kept my gaze straight ahead. "How's the renovation going?" *Keep him distracted.*

"Slow. I was able to get the concrete out of the old pool. I need to fill the gigantic hole in my backyard, but I keep getting calls to sub since it's flu season."

"How's subbing?" All of the checkout lanes were busy, so I chose the line with one woman in it. But she'd crammed her cart with so many artificial flowers, it looked like a rolling bouquet.

"The world of education isn't for me."

"I hear you." The mechanical words came out by habit. Forget Nice Georgia. Even Bad Georgia had vanished.

I was Robot Georgia.

I tightened my grip on the cart and stared at the woman in front of me as if that could make her move faster. How many fake flowers did one person need?

Hamlet rested his hand on my shoulder. "Georgia Rae, I'm not going to ask what's wrong because I can see you don't want me to. And it's none of my business."

The lump that'd spent entirely too much time in my throat resurfaced with a vengeance thanks to the kindness in his voice.

"Please just know that I'm praying for you."

"Thank you," I whispered.

With my bodyguard in tow, I arrived at Harrison Event Center, which was housed in the old Harrison township school. The historic brick building had been repurposed after people protested its demolition. Even though the structure was in the middle of nowhere and surrounded by fields, it was a popular venue for wedding receptions.

As soon as I walked into the gymnasium-turned-banquet-hall, Wanda hurried over to me.

"It's time I let you in on a secret." She pushed her bangs aside.

I took in the tables that'd yet to be decorated and wondered why we were having this conversation now. "What's that?"

She looked over my shoulder. "May I help you, sir?"

"I'm looking after Georgia today." Pat entered and removed his cap and coat.

"Cal hired him," I said. "Pat, Wanda. Wanda, Pat."

"I've got five daughters and survived a wedding for each one," he said. "You need help decorating, let me know." He saluted.

"You may be sorry you offered. Now." She took my arm. "About that secret." With Pat following, she led me out a side door where an Oliver 77 Row Crop tractor was parked behind the building. "Ta-da!"

I stared at the tractor's flawless yellow and green paint that had clearly been restored. "Is this the 1951 Oliver that was sitting in Grandpa's barn?"

She beamed. "Sure is. I had it refurbished as a wedding present."

Enter Lumpy Throat. I was going to give him a name since he was around so much. Louis. Louis the Lump. "That's really thoughtful. Daddy and Grandpa bought it to fix up right before Daddy died, but Grandpa never got around to it."

"Ron wanted to sell it because of the move, but I didn't want him to do that. I had Earl Smith pretend to buy it and then restore it for me. I want to display it at the reception in honor of your daddy, so Earl drove it over this morning." Her face darkened. "Although, after the way he talked to me yesterday morning at Pastry Delight, I'm sorry I hired him instead of someone else."

"I heard."

She grimaced. "I think the whole town heard." She waved a hand. "But most people know not to believe everything they hear from Earl Smith—even his own daughter has told me that."

"He's not invited to the wedding, is he?" I had a mental picture of him jumping up and stopping the wedding.

"Oh heavens, no. We tried to keep the guest list fairly small." She ran her hand over the tractor's seat.

I hugged her. "This is such a thoughtful gift."

We walked back inside.

"I sure hope he's surprised." Wanda smiled. "Beverly knew

and was afraid the secret had gotten out. One afternoon, she called me because she thought Earl was going to spill the beans."

I took off my coat and hung it on the back of a chair. "Wait. Were you talking about that at the museum? Like a week ago Wednesday?"

"Yes." She opened a container full of white pillar candles. "Well, Beverly was there, and we were talking on the phone. She had her hands full chatting with me and trying to flag down the mailman since we had fundraising letters that needed to go out." She tilted her head. "How'd you know about that?"

"One of my friends overheard Beverly talking, and we were afraid it had something to do with her murder, but we didn't know who she was talking to."

"I see." She handed me the candle container. "Start putting these on the tables."

I took it and began distributing the candles onto the mirrors in the center of each table.

"No wonder you were asking questions about the volunteers." Wanda chuckled. "Just so you know, my son took me out to Earl's house to see the progress on the tractor last Thursday night, and I didn't want to say anything because of the surprise. Between that and the NRA envelope, I probably looked mighty guilty." Her eyes shone.

Busted.

"I'm *so* sorry."

"No worries. Your heart's in the right place."

I finished placing the candles and set the container aside. "Did you notice anything unusual going on at Beverly's when you were at Earl's house?"

"No, but we were there well before anything happened. We left about eight or so. Tyler spent the rest of the evening helping me unpack my kitchen." She raised her eyebrows. "I told Detective Hawk the same thing when she talked to me after the fire."

I didn't want to show it, but I felt as if someone had slipped a thousand-pound backpack off my shoulders.

That afternoon, I stepped back and surveyed our handiwork in the chapel at Wildcat Springs Community Church. After we'd finished at the reception hall, Wanda, Pat, and I had moved on to the church where Grandpa had joined us. Having a project had done little to keep my mind off the turmoil with Cal, and every so often, I'd have to stop, take a deep breath, and will away the tears that kept welling in my eyes.

The Winston-Morris clan had done a fine job of decorating in spite of our setbacks. The new batch of trees stood in clusters near the altar and twinkled with the lights.

Grandpa put his arm around me. "Thanks for all your help."

"You're welcome." I glanced around the chapel. Wanda had already left to change for the rehearsal, and we were alone. "Can we talk?"

"Sure."

I sat on the carpeted steps that led to the altar. "Would Earl Smith have any reason to spread rumors about you?"

Grandpa snorted as he sat next to me. "Earl Smith doesn't need a reason to spread rumors other than he flat out enjoys it." He grimaced. "You heard about what he said to Wanda?"

"Yes."

"It hurt her feelings, even though she knew it was a bunch of hooey. Hates having people talking nonsense about her loved ones. I took it with a grain of salt. People who know me realize I'd never hurt your grandma. We did our share of bickering and had a couple of big fights in our marriage, but we never went to bed angry." He looked me straight in the eyes. "And I certainly never laid a hand on her."

"I know. She'd have thumped you back good if you had."

He chuckled. "That's true. As for secrets in the past, the worst I can think of was that Earl, some other guys on our high school basketball team, and I got a hold of some of his dad's beer one night and drank too much. We egged a few houses."

I giggled.

"It wasn't so funny when my dad found out a few days later and blistered my hind end with a switch. I stayed away from Earl after that."

"Why would he make stuff up?"

"Too much time on his hands. Plus, I think he's still sweet on Wanda. I'd venture to say he thinks I swooped in on his territory."

"Did they ever date?"

"Nope. She told me he never bothered to ask her, but she wasn't interested. Said it would've been too strange with Earl being her daughter-in-law's dad. Could be he regrets not sticking his neck out. I'm sure glad *I* took a chance."

I ran my hand over the carpeted step. "How'd you know you wanted to marry Wanda?"

"I asked God about what he thought, and he gave me peace about going ahead."

Peace from God. Did I have that in my relationship with Cal? It'd been there when we'd started dating, but now I wasn't so sure.

Grandpa patted me on the back and stood. "I wouldn't have moved forward without it."

"It turns out Beverly was helping Wanda with Grandpa's wedding present," I shouted from my bedroom, where I was slipping into dressy black pants. My voice was still raspy from the smoke inhalation.

"Good," Brandi said from my living room. "I feel terrible for putting doubt in your mind."

Since I'd forgotten to bring clothes for the rehearsal dinner to Mom and Dan's house, Pat had escorted me to my place so I could change. After checking the house, he was waiting outside in his minivan and would be relieved of his duties as soon as Cal met me at the rehearsal dinner.

Brandi had stopped by with a plate of fresh snickerdoodles. I hadn't filled her in on my tiff with Cal since I didn't want to start crying and ruin my makeup. Plus, I wasn't ready to analyze everything that'd happened.

I pulled a black sweater with silver threads over my head and stepped out of my bedroom. Brandi lounged on my couch rustling through the latest issue of *People* magazine. Gus lay on his back with his feet in the air. I'd have to keep him away from me unless I wanted dog hair all over my pants.

"You had to say something about what you overheard. What if it'd turned out to be important?" I flipped my hair out of the back of my sweater.

Brandi shut the magazine and tossed it onto my coffee table along with the latest copy of *Farm Journal*. "That outfit's cute."

"Thanks." I stepped into my black pumps.

"Something else is bothering you."

I nodded as I sat on the opposite end of the sectional. "How'd you know Brian was the one? Did you know all of a sudden? Did it take a long time? Did you jump in and hope he was the right one?"

She crossed her legs. "I don't believe there's only one person out there for you. There are many people with whom you could have a wonderful marriage. God brings possibilities into your life and gives you the wisdom to make a good choice."

It wasn't the most romantic notion, but I agreed. I'd never been a fan of the whole soul mate concept, because what if your soul mate got flattened by a semi or married someone else? Were you doomed to walk through life single because one person made a mistake? God was a lot bigger than that.

"How'd you know Brian was a good choice?"

"I prayed about it. Then, one weekend I caught that horrible norovirus that swept through the school—we even had to close for a couple of days because so many kids were sick. The health department came in and cleaned everything."

I wrinkled my nose. "Yeah. I remember hearing about that." Brandi and I hadn't been hanging out at the time.

"Anyway, Brian risked life and limb to come take care of me. He didn't care if it meant he might get sick. He put on gloves and a mask and charged into my apartment to make sure I was okay. Even though I was puking my guts out, I knew he loved me if he was willing to take care of me like that—when he didn't have to."

"Brian was a great guy."

"I know." She met my gaze. "Promise me you'll hold out for God's best and never settle for good enough."

I wrapped my arms around my waist. "I promise."

CHAPTER EIGHTEEN

When I was in college, my voice professor smoked cigarettes. None of his students could truly believe the sheer hypocrisy coming from a man who lectured us about the necessity of preserving our singing voices, but it was true.

Once, as a joke, a few of my fellow music majors had sneaked into his office and plastered his desk chair with articles about the harm smoking does to the voice.

I might or might not have played a role as lookout.

Professor Conlon was not amused—though nothing had ever come of the incident, because I was certain he'd known we were right.

Honestly, I had no idea how he ever managed to sing, and his habit never seemed to affect his vocal cords. I was a wimp of grand proportions, because when I sang "How Beautiful" during the rehearsal, my raw voice cracked twice.

I'd be taking a vow of silence and chugging lots of honey-laced tea between tonight and tomorrow's ceremony at four-thirty. Well, as much as Georgia Rae Winston could stay silent. For once, I might learn more by listening than speaking.

When I finished singing, I retreated to the church pew where I watched Pastor Mark walk Grandpa and Wanda through the ceremony.

Cal slipped in and sat beside me. "Pat said you were a good girl today."

I snickered. "I *do* know how to behave."

He put his arm around me. "How're you feeling?"

"Fine. My voice is a mess, so starting now, I'm done talking until after I sing at the wedding."

He nodded, but I detected a flicker of annoyance in his eyes. Maybe I was being paranoid. After all, it wasn't like I *wanted* to be silent. That wasn't exactly my strong suit.

I removed my phone and opened a note-taking app.

Any leads on the fire that you're allowed to share?

He leaned over and whispered, "Wanda was at the church talking with the wedding coordinator. Earl couldn't have set the barn fire because after he left the bakery, he had a dental appointment. I verified it with Dr. Burke's office."

Apparently, Earl was just a jealous liar. At least I wasn't living next to a murdering pyromaniac.

"Taryn Anderson called and left a message after we left the bakery. Said she remembered that before Earl talked to Wanda, he visited with his buddy Dwight."

Dwight Winters from the museum?

"Yep. Dwight left right before Wanda sat at Earl's table." He glanced around. "Also, Mallory Morris was there picking up an order for the school office, and Fiona Sylvan was there getting a bear claw."

All while Wanda was on the phone with me talking about the trees?

"Yep. Mallory and Fiona aren't exactly buddies, and as Taryn said, 'They gave each other the stink eye.'"

The women had run in the same circle during high school. What had happened? This whole situation was getting more twisted by the minute. I shook my head.

"We'll figure it out." He looked around the room at my family members who'd begun filtering in.

Aunt Rhonda slid into the pew next to Cal and extended her hand. "Rhonda Thompson. Georgia's aunt. I've been *dying* to meet you."

He shook her hand. "Cal Perkins. And I'm glad it didn't come to that."

I choked back a laugh.

Puzzlement reigned in her expression for a second. Then she emitted a hearty chuckle. "Good one, Detective." She pointed at me. "I could tell you stories about this one."

Please don't. But part of me was thankful for her interruption that eased the tension.

Cal surveyed me with gleaming eyes. "What have you got on her?"

I opened my mouth to protest and remembered my vow of silence. I narrowed my eyes.

"Well, one summer, she and her brother came to Indy to stay with my husband Gary and me while Ray and Jill went on a trip to Maine to see lighthouses. Anyway, Dakota and my son Eric were angels as usual, but I always had to keep an eye on Georgia and my daughter Michelle. How they could cook up so much trouble was beyond me, but they did." Aunt Rhonda waved a hand. "One time I caught them launching their baby dolls off our treehouse. Can you believe that? Little girls who ought to have a nurturing side were chucking those poor dollies to the ground. I'd expect that from boys, but girls? I'd have never dreamed of doing that when I was a little kid. I guess it didn't turn out to be that big of a deal because Michelle has a baby boy of her own and hasn't dropped him on his head. Jury's still out on Georgia."

My face had to look like a pomegranate. *Vow of silence. Vow of silence. Vow of silence!*

Cal opened his mouth, but Aunt Rhonda wasn't finished.

"Then there was the time I caught them playing beauty salon. Would you believe they cut the hair off their Totally Hair Barbies?"

"I could see how that'd be tempting," Cal said, somehow managing to keep a straight face.

Aunt Rhonda shook her head. "Then they decided they wanted to be like those TV chefs and have their own cooking show. Ruined a perfectly good chicken, a skillet, and my favorite spatula. I had to call the fire department. The worst part? That incident scared the two of them out of the kitchen for life. Jill tried her best to get this one"—she pointed at me again, and I decided I should change my name to This One Winston— "into 4-H, but that was a *disaster*. Michelle isn't any better in the kitchen, so thank goodness her husband knows how to cook." She blinked at Cal. "Can you cook?"

"Yes, ma'am. I enjoy it."

"Oh, thank goodness." She waved a hand. "I take comfort in knowing my niece won't starve if she marries you." She patted Cal on the shoulder and glanced toward our family members that were migrating toward the sanctuary exit. "It was great meeting you. I'd better go find my hubby because it looks like they're ready for us to head to the restaurant for dinner. I'm starving, and I'd be willing to bet you are too." She turned to me and whispered, "You've picked a good one. Don't mess things up." Then she sauntered away.

I folded my hands on my lap and stared at the decorative trees.

Cal leaned over and whispered, "Now I know where you get your talking ability."

Grandpa hadn't had much say in the wedding plans but had put his foot down when it was time to decide where the rehearsal dinner would be. June's Family Restaurant was his favorite, so that's where the festivities would occur. June's was known throughout Richard County for fried chicken, so that's what we'd be having, along with noodles, mashed potatoes, green beans, corn, dinner rolls, and assorted pies for dessert.

When Cal and I entered the banquet room, there were two long tables covered with blue-checkered tablecloths. Several containers of apple butter and Amish peanut butter spread dotted the tables. Next to the wall, a table laden with slices of apple, peach, peanut butter, cream, and cherry pies beckoned us.

I scanned the room in search of seats, and the only place with two remaining places was across from Tyler and Mallory Morris. I led Cal to the table, and we joined them.

"Georgia is resting her voice tonight so she's in top shape to sing at the wedding tomorrow," Cal said.

Mallory shot me a sympathetic look. "Is she sick?"

"No. She's healing from mild smoke inhalation from a barn fire yesterday."

Mallory furrowed her brow and turned to me. "One of your barns?"

"No. It was the barn on Beverly Alspaugh's property," Cal said. "Georgia was picking up decorations Aunt Beverly had made for the wedding when someone shut her in the barn and set it on fire."

Mallory gasped. "How awful!" Her eyes widened. "Is that the same fire that killed Clara Alspaugh?"

"Yes," he said.

"My goodness. I didn't know anyone else was involved. Normally, I slip into the high school library to read the newspaper, but today was insane, so I didn't get a chance. We had a couple of boys get in a fight, and that was the first one all year, and the assistant principal was out, so I had to take care of everything. I'm Mallory, by the way."

Cal extended his hand over the table. "Cal Perkins, Georgia's boyfriend."

Mallory grasped his hand. "Pleasure to meet you."

She put a little too much emphasis on the word *pleasure*.

"This is my husband, Tyler. Wanda's his mom." She pointed at a middle-aged man and woman who were engrossed in entertaining a toddler. "That's Tyler's brother Todd and his wife Kelly from Tennessee—and their grandson Liam." When they looked up, I smiled and waved. We'd met at my church's Christmas program a couple of months ago.

Both Tyler and Todd had inherited their square jaws from their dad Paul, but years of marriage to Mallory probably explained the defeated expression in Tyler's eyes that was absent from his brother's.

Tyler extended his hand to Cal. "Nice to meet you."

Mallory leaned forward. "Tell me what you do for a living, Cal."

"I'm a detective with the Richard County Sheriff's Department."

Mallory pressed her hand over her cleavage. "Are you investigating Beverly's murder?"

"Yes, ma'am."

Mallory shook her head. "It's so awful. I taught with Beverly for years before she retired. She was such a nice lady, and I know how much she meant to my mother-in-law. I'm sure you'll find who did it. You look very capable."

Merciful heavens. Mallory had definitely emphasized the word capable. In front of her husband. I nudged Cal's foot under the table, and he tapped back.

Thankfully, the waitresses began bringing steaming bowls of food. My eyes fell on the platter of chicken, and my stomach rumbled. For the next few minutes we focused on passing the serving dishes and platters.

Tyler struck up a conversation about baseball with Cal, and he looked happier than he had all evening.

"Do you follow baseball?" Mallory asked.

I shook my head.

"I don't either. I'm a basketball girl." She rested her fork on her plate that contained a small amount of mashed potatoes and a single chicken wing. "I tell you. I've been sick over what happened to Clara. We got to be friends during her senior year after she had a falling out with Fiona Ford—well—it's Sylvan now."

I reached for my phone.

What caused the falling out?

She dabbed her lips with her napkin. "Fiona tried to steal your dad away from Clara."

My eyes widened.

"Oh, yes. Fiona knew a good thing when she saw it, but Ray was loyal to Clara and didn't encourage her. Still, Clara didn't want anything to do with her after that. I can't say that I blame her. I'd have done the same if she'd tried that stunt with Tyler."

Before I could protest that Clara and Fiona must've worked things out since they'd kept in touch after Clara left town, Mallory squealed and jumped up.

"Excuse me. My son and daughter-in-law finally made it here with my new granddaughter!" She flitted across the banquet room to the young man and woman standing in the doorway holding a baby carrier.

While Tyler and Cal continued baseball talk, I pushed mashed potatoes and noodles around my plate and wondered if we'd ever find the truth in this situation.

CHAPTER NINETEEN

Grandpa and Wanda's wedding day dawned clear and cold. As I scrambled around Mom's guest room in my robe getting ready for my hair appointment at ten, I kept thinking about Cal. After the rehearsal dinner the night before, he'd given me a kiss and followed me back to Mom and Dan's house.

But even though our relationship seemed fine on the surface, I felt tension building underneath.

Was it because of Hamlet? I turned on my blow dryer. I hadn't asked Hamlet to come to Bible study. That was all on Evan. If Cal didn't like Hamlet being there, then it was time for him to get over his phobia of small groups and show up. I'd invited him multiple times.

I'd reassured him that nobody would make him share anything that made him feel uncomfortable, and we didn't get that deep anyway. If I had a concern that was highly personal, I wouldn't share it in mixed company. That's what Brandi and Ashley were for.

I'd let the issue go because Cal was such a good boyfriend in other ways, but if our relationship got any more serious, I'd have to make a choice about my church attendance, and that meant going to Cal's church. He'd made it clear he had no intention of attending Wildcat Springs Community. It was too big, and the worship was too contemporary for his taste.

The fact that I hadn't started attending with him—at least sometimes—made me wonder about my own level of commitment. What was holding me back? Was it that I'd attended my church since I was a month old?

Or were church and Hamlet just symptoms of a bigger problem that Cal sensed too?

Was that why he'd put an offer on a house? The only other explanation was that he wanted to prove he could buy a house and he didn't need mine.

I didn't like either option.

"You have nice hair." Fiona donned her red glasses, picked up my locks, and surveyed them while I sat in the chair at her salon. "Walk Like an Egyptian" played over the sound system, and I tapped my foot to the beat.

Pat lounged on a couch near the door and was flipping through a beat-up copy of *Cosmopolitan*.

Merciful heavens.

I'd already shown Fiona my phone with a message about why I wasn't talking, so I mouthed, "Thank you."

"What would you like me to do?" She spun me around so I faced the mirror.

I tapped my phone and showed her a picture of a curly up-do I'd found a couple of days ago.

Fiona pursed her lips and studied it. "I can work with that. Your hair's so thick that I may have to modify a couple of things, but it shouldn't be a problem."

I gave her a thumbs up, and she patted me on the shoulder.

"How are you doing? After the fire and all?"

I typed my answer.

Okay. You? I know you and Clara were friends.

Fiona brushed my hair. "I'm hanging in there. We'd been buddies since third grade when we both were in Mrs. Cooper's class. I was pretty shy as a kid, and Clara decided we were going to be friends one day during recess, and that was that."

I caught her eye in the mirror and gave her a sympathetic smile.

"I thought you'd be lost without talking, but your face and eyes say it all." She sprayed a section of my hair and wound it around a curling iron. "I'd been trying to convince Clara to come home for years, and I feel awful that when she finally listened, she got killed." She released the curl and sprayed another section of hair.

Did she ever tell you why she never visited?

"No. I tried to get it out of her, but she always shut me down. Before she left, there were some awful rumors about her. There was speculation that she ran away because she was pregnant, and her family was ashamed. Some people said the kid was your dad's, and he didn't want to claim it. I had trouble believing that one because I heard him say once he didn't believe in fooling around outside of marriage, and he would've claimed any baby of his. Others said Clara was so wild she didn't even know who the father was. She and your daddy fought on prom night, and she didn't have a thing to do with him after that. Graduation was a week later, and she left for Texas the day after."

Did her leaving have anything to do with something that happened at an after-party on prom night?

"Could've been, but I don't know for sure. My parents wouldn't let me go to any after-parties, but even though Clara and I were in the same group that went to prom together, we didn't spend much time together senior year. Halfway through, Clara dropped me like a hot potato and started running around with Mallory Smith—well you know her as Mallory Morris. It was Mallory this, Mallory that." Her face twisted.

Was it because Fiona had tried to steal Daddy from Clara?

Did you and Clara have a fight over boys or something?

"Nope. It would've made sense if we had, but we didn't have the same taste. I liked the brooding musician type—not the jocks. My first husband was a drummer in a rock band. Then the jerk left me for a groupie."

If Fiona didn't like jocks, then why had she begun an affair with Jack Schultz? Unless she was over brooding musicians because of her divorce.

"I always figured Clara picked Mallory because she was more popular than me and liked to party. Plus, she had a fancy car, and I didn't. Lot of good it did her. She wrapped the thing around a tree. Anyway. That's all water under the bridge, but to this day, I'm not a Mallory Morris fan. Eventually, I found other gals to run around with, which was good, because if I hadn't, Clara would've left me high and dry when she moved."

How did you start talking again?

"Years later she sent a letter out of the blue, and I was willing to let bygones be bygones." She curled another section of my hair.

"We talked on the phone a couple of times a year." She released my hair, set the curling iron aside, and looked me straight in the eye. "Speaking of letters coming out of the blue. I just remembered something." She shook her head. "I can't believe I forgot all about this."

I raised my eyebrows.

"Years ago, I got roped into serving on the football state championship reunion committee with your dad, and about a week before he died, he asked me for Clara's address because he wanted to write her."

I started to type, but she waved her hand.

"He didn't say why, and I didn't ask. But it seemed like he had something important on his mind, and I figured with the reunion bringing back all those high school memories, he wanted to encourage her to come home and visit."

Did Clara ever say if she received a letter?

"No. She didn't say, but I think if she had, she'd have told me when we talked after Ray died." She sprayed my hair. "Evidently he took what he wanted to say to his grave."

Goosebumps rose on my arms.

With my hair finally coiffed to perfection and Pat as my faithful escort, I left Sassy Salon and drove to Ashley's house for lunch with her and Brandi. I didn't need to be at the church until around three, so that gave me plenty of time to catch up with my friends.

Or at least listen while the two of them talked.

I waved at Pat in his van and walked around to Ashley's back door.

"It's unlocked!" she shouted.

When I entered, the scent of chicken broth filled her kitchen. I smiled and waved, having already warned her about my vow of silence.

"I made chicken noodle soup. It might be good for your throat." She pointed a spoon at the kitchen table where a plate of crackers and mini chicken salad sandwiches waited. "And tea with honey, so drink up." She brought me a cup.

I took my place at the table as Brandi entered.

She pushed her hood off. "How long until spring?"

"Approximately twenty-five days, hon." Ashley pointed toward the calendar hanging on the side of her cabinet.

Brandi laughed as she took off her coat and glanced toward the calendar. "That was rhetorical, but you actually have a count-down." She joined me at the table.

Ashley ladled two bowls of soup and gave them to Brandi and me. When she returned from the stove with her own bowl, she was beaming. She placed the bowl on the table and clasped her hands. "I gave my two-week's notice yesterday."

Brandi and I looked at each other.

Ashley's smile melted away. "You can't possibly be surprised. I told you I was going to quit." She sat, shook out her napkin, and placed it on her lap. "I thought you'd be happy for me. This is a big step."

I gave her a thumbs up.

"How about I bless the food?" Brandi said.

We bowed our heads, and she prayed.

"Now," Brandi said to Ashley. "Tell us more about where you are in your business preparations."

"Yesterday, I signed a lease on the building. I'm allowed to make changes, so I want to update the restrooms and improve the lighting."

I grabbed my phone.

Let us know if you need help painting.

Ashley nodded. "I will. There are several things I need to do myself to keep the cost down."

"Have you told your parents yet?" Brandi asked.

Ashley ducked her head. "No."

Brandi arched an eyebrow. "When do you plan to do this?"

"Soon."

"I'll be praying about that conversation." Brandi took a sip of soup.

Ashley stirred her soup. "Thanks."

I sensed the need for a subject change.

J.T. update?

Ashley rested her spoon on a plate. "We had the best time the other night. The movie was a total dud, so we walked out and went for coffee—and closed the place down."

I clapped.

"I've always known J.T. was a good guy, but it impresses me that he's such a hard worker. He comes across as so laid back, but he was telling me he earned another cruise to the Bahamas because his sales were so good."

I hadn't heard that yet, but I was proud of my cousin.

"When's the next date?" Brandi asked.

"There's not going to be one."

I dropped my spoon, tapped an angry-face emoji onto my phone, and held it up.

"Explain." Brandi crossed her arms.

Ashley stared at her hands. "The timing is terrible. I need to focus on my art studio. I don't have time for a new relationship."

"What'd J.T. say?" Brandi asked before I could type the same question.

"He understands. He's willing to be patient."

"For how long? You can't lead him on indefinitely."

"I'm not leading him on," Ashley said. "I've been very clear about my inability to commit."

"Are you sure this is about the studio and not about you being gun shy because of your broken engagement?" Brandi studied her.

Ashley had been on many dates but hadn't let herself get into a serious relationship since her fiancé had walked out on their wedding day.

"Yes. Besides, it's not like J.T. and I aren't going to see each other. He's offered to help me fix up the studio, and there's Bible study." She put a chicken salad sandwich on her plate. "New topic."

I sipped my tea. I wanted so badly to be able to talk to my friends about Cal. I needed their input about my confusion. They could reassure me that I was being paranoid. That the bad feeling in my gut was just me projecting past experiences onto my current situation.

"My sister-in-law set me up with a guy from their church," Brandi said. "She's been after me for a while, and she finally convinced me."

I typed a softball emoji with a question mark.

Brandi laughed. "We'll have to work around my schedule. His name is Dalton, and he's a physical therapist in Richardville."

"When are you going out?" Ashley sat up straighter.

"Tonight."

"Do you need help with your outfit?" Ashley asked.

"That'd be great."

I tucked away the rest of my soup while they scrutinized Brandi's wardrobe. I'd have to rely on God to help the turmoil in my soul.

I'm sorry. I'm tied up with a case. I may not get to the wedding. I'll try to make the reception.

Tears pricked my eyes as I read Cal's message. I'd wanted him to hear me sing. I set my phone on my dresser and plunked down on the edge of my bed. Since Pat was stationed outside in his van, I'd decided it was safe to hang out at home until it was time for the wedding. I was thankful for the privacy, but I missed Gus, who was still at Mom and Dan's.

Lord, please show me your will with Cal.

I gazed out the window at my pond, which had developed a thin layer of ice. The morning sunshine had disappeared behind a thick layer of clouds. According to the forecasts, we were supposed to get snow flurries that night—though nothing bad enough to put a damper on the wedding festivities.

Kicking off my shoes, I sat on my bed, being careful not to damage my hair. Tears spilled over. For Daddy. For Grandma Winston. For Beverly.

And for everything I feared was coming.

When my sobs subsided, I stared at the ceiling. I needed to put cold spoons over my eyes, warm up my voice, and get dressed. I hauled myself off the bed.

Too bad I didn't have a happy face hanging in my closet.

I arrived at the church and went straight to the chapel for a sound check. Pat slid into a pew in the back of the room.

Hamlet waved at me from the sound booth. "Devin has the flu, so he called me to take over."

Of course. Why couldn't I get away from this man? At least

he was wearing a dark gray suit instead of a sweater vest. Masking my dismay, I showed him my phone with my standard vow-of-silence message.

"Would you like to practice your song?"

I gave him a thumbs up, grabbed a microphone, and walked to the stage. A few minutes later, the pressure lifted. Though my pipes weren't in top form, my lack of talking had done wonders to heal them, and my voice hadn't cracked once.

Hamlet applauded. "That was beautiful. Your Grandpa will be proud."

Pat gave me a thumbs-up.

"Thank you," I mouthed as I wandered to the back of the chapel and sat in a pew. I couldn't quite bring myself to enter the bridal room. I'd peeked in earlier, and Mallory had been fluttering around helping Wanda into her dress. Aunt Rhonda and Michelle were providing moral support and representing our side of the family. Knowing Beverly should be there and wasn't stabbed my heart.

"Are you okay?" Hamlet asked.

I made the so-so motion.

"May I pray for you?"

I nodded.

Hamlet slid into the pew and bowed his head. "Father, help Georgia through whatever's troubling her. Let her know she has many people who care about her. Make her voice sound as beautiful as it did during practice. Amen."

I swallowed over the lump in my throat, reached over, and squeezed his hand in thanks.

"Georgia?" Cal stood in the chapel entrance. "What's going on?"

CHAPTER TWENTY

I scurried over to give Cal a hug—or at least as fast as I could move in my silver shoes with three-inch heels that had me looking eye-to-eye with him for the first time ever.

"Hey, Hamlet." Cal eyed Hamlet, who hovered behind me. "Is everything okay? I obviously walked in on something."

Hamlet shook his head. "Your girlfriend is upset, though she couldn't tell me why because of her vow of silence, so I prayed. No big deal."

"Do you have to keep up this vow of silence?" Cal asked.

I nodded.

"It paid off," Hamlet said. "Her voice sounded lovely in the warm-up."

For about two seconds, I thought Cal was going to deck him. Instead, he put his arm around my waist. "Thanks for taking care of her."

We waved goodbye to Pat, and Cal led me outside of the chapel where the first few guests were lining up to sign the guest book. Inside, the pianist began playing as we headed toward the café.

"You look beautiful, by the way. That dress . . . wow."

I smiled at him. I'd hoped he'd like the dress. It was fitted, falling to my knee. Sequins added some sparkle to the all-over, dark blue lace. My favorite part was the long sleeves—perfect for winter and hiding my pasty arms.

Maybe I didn't need to worry about my relationship with Cal. He'd made it to the wedding. He cared enough to get a body-guard. I'd accused Ashley of projecting her fears from past relationships onto her current one when I was guilty of that very thing. I took my phone from my silver clutch and started typing.

Is everything okay at work?

"Yes. It's been a crazy day. We finally have a positive ID for the body the construction workers found a couple of weeks ago, and I needed to be there for the press conference."

Who was it?

"Keith Jefferson. His father and sister are relieved to have closure, since they've been living without answers for thirty-eight years. Unfortunately, Keith's mother died last year."

Would my family have to wait that long to find out what happened to Daddy? Or would we die without answers? I stared out the café windows at the parking lot. More and more guests were streaming in.

Cal studied me. "Do you want to go in and have a seat, so you don't have to talk to everyone?"

I gave three emphatic nods, and we returned to the chapel where my brother Dakota headed straight for us. Because it was tax season, he and his wife Stella hadn't been able to make it to the rehearsal, but Dakota had assured Wanda that he'd been an usher for five weddings and was an expert.

Like me, Dakota was tall. We shared the same brown eyes and honey-colored hair, though he'd inherited his features from my mom's side of the family. In fact, Dakota and J.T. looked more like brothers than first cousins, except Dakota wore dark-framed glasses.

Dakota hugged me and then held out his hand to Cal, whom he'd met at Christmas. "Cal. Good to see you again, man."

"Likewise."

Dakota pointed to a pew at the front of the church. "I'll take you up, so you can sit with Stella." He held out his arm. "Mom told us you aren't talking until after you sing, which I told her I'd have to see to believe."

I raised my eyebrows as we moved down the center aisle. The florist had finished the decorations, and bunches of white and pink roses adorned the ends of the pews.

"Now I believe it." He leaned over. "Will your wedding be next?" he whispered.

I shrugged. I should've started collecting money from each person who asked me that, because I'd have a nice little nest egg by now. Enough for my own escape-the-nasty-Indiana-weather excursion.

"I need to know if I should vet this guy or not. He was pretty quiet at Christmas. I'm never too sure about the quiet ones." He stopped next to our pew.

Spoken like a true Winston.

I turned to give Stella a hug. Her petite frame reminded me of my mom's build, though Stella had waist-length black hair that was shiny enough to be in a shampoo commercial.

"Are you nervous about singing?" she whispered.

I shook my head.

"That's good. I'd be passed out in the bathroom." She brushed lint from the sleeve of her red sheath dress. "Hey, Cal." She waved.

"Hey." He removed his buzzing phone from his pocket. "Excuse me, ladies. I need to take this call." He strode up the aisle.

"Are you guys next?" Stella glanced over her shoulder.

I shrugged and smoothed my dress's hem. Why had Cal stepped out? Was he going to leave?

"Excuse me," I mouthed and slipped out of my seat to follow him.

Mom and Dan gave me puzzled looks as I passed. The chapel had filled with guests—mostly family and a few of Grandpa and Wanda's close friends. When I reached the multi-purpose room, I found Cal on his phone, facing the corner near the coffee bar. I edged closer.

"Now's not the time to tell them." He paused. "I know. You're right." He squeezed the bridge of his nose. "I'll handle it as soon as I can. Thanks, Vanessa." He disconnected.

"Handle what? What's wrong?"

Surprise flickered in his eyes as he faced me and pressed his lips together. "Let's go back inside. The wedding's about to start." He pointed to the sanctuary door.

"You had a break in Beverly's case, didn't you?"

He arched an eyebrow. "I see you've given up on your vow of silence."

"At this point, it's not going to make much difference." I'd be done singing in twenty minutes.

"I see." He rested his hand on my shoulder. "We'll talk after the ceremony."

The anguish in his eyes caused my stomach to plummet. "You know who killed Beverly."

He looked away. "No. We don't." He stalked toward the chapel. "But we do have a new lead. I promise I'll fill you in. Just not now."

I glanced around the empty room. "Please tell me," I whispered.

He stopped, put both hands on my arms, and looked into my eyes. "Georgia, you're going to have to trust me that it's best to have this conversation after the wedding."

I ran my thumb back and forth over my purse. "Okay."

Trust. Why was that so hard for me?

We returned to the chapel in silence.

CHAPTER TWENTY-ONE

As Cal and I scooted into the pew, Grandpa and Pastor Mark took their places at the front. Behind them, the white trees sparkled in the dim light. Cal grasped my hand and squeezed it.

The pianist played "Great is Thy Faithfulness," and we stood as Wanda walked down the aisle between her sons Tyler and Todd.

Wanda's silver, floor-length gown shimmered. She carried a bouquet of pink and white roses with silver accents. I turned my gaze to Grandpa, who was beaming.

Would Cal ever look at me that way? Did I still want him to? The thought struck me so hard, I had to grab the back of the pew in front of me.

"You may be seated," Pastor Mark said.

I shot Cal a weak smile, and he reached for my hand.

"What a joyous day for the Morris and Winston families. I never cease to be amazed when God brings two people together."

Was God bringing me together with Cal? Or was he warning

me not to move ahead? I touched the necklace Cal had given me for my birthday.

"Instead of having a small, private ceremony, Wanda and Ron opted to have a wedding because they wanted to celebrate the joining of their families. We'll begin with scripture, which Ron's granddaughter Michelle will read."

I couldn't bring myself to focus as Michelle read from Ephesians five. My eyes fell on Dakota, who was gripping Stella's hand. They'd met in college, but I'd never asked my brother when he'd known he wanted to marry her.

Cal nudged me. "You're up."

Michelle was moving back to her seat. When I approached the front of the chapel, a tiny wave of apprehension vibrated in my gut. I loved performing, but nervousness always hit me at the last second.

The music began, and I launched into the opening bars of "How Beautiful." As I sang the chorus, I caught Hamlet's eye. He smiled, and it was clear he was enjoying my performance. I glanced at my boyfriend, who sat stone-faced.

Was it because of the news he'd received? Or did he not like my voice—or me anymore?

———

After the ceremony ended, Cal and I worked our way through the receiving line and congratulated Grandpa and Wanda. Then, I dragged Cal away from the crowd toward the offices. "Now will you tell me what's going on?"

"Yes." He waved Dakota and Stella over to where we were standing next to the coatracks.

"What're you—?"

"Hey," Cal said as they approached. "I need to talk to you

and your sister. I'd like your mom and stepdad to be in on it too. Have you seen them?"

Concern flickered in Dakota's expression. "What's this about?"

"I'll tell you in a minute." Cal's tone left no room for argument.

Dakota and I exchanged glances.

"I'll find them." Stella walked away, her hair swishing.

"Let's find an empty Sunday school room," Dakota said.

"Oh, Georgia, you sounded beautiful." Mallory Morris flitted over to us. "No one would ever know you suffered from smoke inhalation. Your voice was as clear as a bell."

"Thank you."

"Why, Dakota Winston." She turned to my brother and gave him the once over. "Look at you. All grown up and handsome. What're you doing these days?" She tilted her head and batted her eyes.

"I'm a CPA." He jingled some change in his pocket. "And I'm married," he added quickly.

"Lucky girl. I saw her sitting with you. She's absolutely gorgeous. Such perfect hair." Mallory flipped her shoulder-length hair. "I never could grow mine that long, so I envy any girl who can. Oh well. God gave me great legs instead."

I coughed. Great legs that she wasn't afraid to show off in that short dress of hers.

"It was nice seeing you again, Mrs. Morris." Dakota turned toward Cal. "You follow college basketball?"

"Sure do," Cal said.

"You can call me Mallory now." She took the hint and sauntered away.

"Not in this lifetime," Dakota muttered.

Stella, Mom, and Dan approached, and Cal led the way to an

empty Sunday school room, and the memory of our argument in one of these classrooms resurfaced.

He'd hated my involvement in the youth pastor's murder investigation and hadn't appreciated all the questions I'd been asking.

We entered the room where Cal and I had fought, and I shut the door behind us.

He motioned to the table in the middle of the room. "Please have a seat."

"What's this about?" Mom asked as she sat in the chair Dan pulled out for her.

"I'm sorry to interrupt your celebration, but Georgia overheard part of my conversation with Detective Hawk earlier, so I wanted to tell you we have a new lead."

"About Beverly Alspaugh's case?" Confusion played in Dan's expression as he asked the question I was sure we were all thinking.

Then, understanding dawned in my mind, and my breath caught. The cases couldn't be connected, could they? But why else would Cal be talking to *us* instead of Beverly's family? Why else would he refuse to tell me *before* the wedding?

"Yes." Cal folded his hands and rested them on the table. "We've received the ballistics report from Beverly's murder."

"And?" My voice wavered.

Cal met my eyes. "The same gun that killed Beverly was used to kill Ray Winston."

CHAPTER TWENTY-TWO

"You'll figure it out, Georgia Rae. God has something special planned for you."

Those weren't Daddy's very last words to me, but it was something he'd said during the final meaningful conversation we'd had that long weekend of fall break during my senior year in college. I'd been in the middle of student teaching and had discovered that my passion for playing piano and singing didn't translate to teaching music.

My elementary school placement had been particularly trying, because I was convinced if one more kiddo tattled about something insipid, I was going to have a tantrum that would send them to the principal for refuge.

And I didn't care.

But my Winston family pride—and lots of prayers—had helped me persevere and graduate with a degree in music education.

"Georgia?" Cal's voice ripped me back to the present and into the Sunday school room. For the second time in less than two weeks, I'd zoned out in front of him. I hadn't scared him off yet, but this might do it.

Dan had his arm around Mom, and she dabbed tears with his handkerchief. Dakota and Stella held hands. Clearly, everyone was eager for answers, and the last thing I wanted was to be the reason for a hold up. "Sorry. Go on." I pressed my hands together to stop the shaking.

"She's as white as a sheet," Stella murmured as she dug around in her sequined clutch. She produced a roll of chewy mints and slid them across the table. "Have some sugar."

"Thanks." With my trembling fingers, I popped a mint from the package and slipped it into my mouth.

"Are you sure you're okay?" Cal's eyes blazed with concern, and he reached over and took my hand.

"Yeah." I ignored my feelings and focused on the facts. "Why would the murderer be dumb enough to use the same gun twice? Why not get rid of it? Hasn't this person ever watched *CSI*?"

"Excellent questions, and I'll do everything I can to get answers." Cal stroked his thumb across my hand and then looked at everyone.

"We have to tell Grandpa," I said.

"No way." Dakota shook his head. "Let him enjoy the reception. He's not been this happy since Grandma died. We can't ruin his wedding day."

"I agree," Mom said.

Dan held up his hands. "I'll stay out of this one."

Of course Dan wouldn't take sides. "Grandpa deserves answers too."

"And he'll have them." Dakota crossed his arms. "We can tell him tomorrow before he leaves for Florida."

My brother was right, but whether we told Grandpa today or tomorrow, this revelation would be forever tied to his wedding. "Fine. We'll wait." We just had to make it through the reception.

Cal looked around the table. "I need you to think about any additional connections between Beverly and Ray that we might not know about."

We all glanced around the table in silence.

"Other than Ray's high school relationship with Beverly's daughter?" Mom asked. "I wish I knew. Beverly was our neighbor for years. A good friend." She shook her head, and tears filled her eyes. "None of this makes any sense."

A knock broke the silence.

"Georgia Rae? Dakota? Are you in there? We need you for pictures." Aunt Rhonda opened the door and peeked in. "What on Earth is going on?"

I hopped up. "We're coming. Sorry. We were talking about what to get Preston and Austin for their birthday in a few weeks." It was a lame excuse, but there was no way we could let Aunt Rhonda know if we wanted to keep this news from Grandpa. I hoped everyone in the room would follow my lead—especially since they were the ones who didn't want to tell.

Aunt Rhonda frowned. "You had to do this in a secret meeting? Why?"

Like aunt, like niece.

Dan studied his Italian loafers, and Mom looked like she was about two seconds from cracking.

"They have friends everywhere, so we have to keep our discussions on the down low if we want to surprise them." Dakota caught my eye.

"They sure do." Dan shoved his hands in his pockets. "Those boys of mine have never known a stranger."

Stella coughed, and Cal's face remained expressionless.

Aunt Rhonda flipped her piercing gaze back and forth between Dakota and me. "Well, we're not getting any younger."

"We're coming," I said. "Sorry for the delay."

Grandpa loved his restored Oliver 77 Row Crop tractor. After pictures, Tyler had hurried ahead to the event center and moved the tractor near the entrance. Our families waited in the foyer until Grandpa and Wanda arrived in their limo, and then we'd rushed outside. I'd taken several great candid shots of Grandpa's surprised expression. With tears shining in his eyes, he'd kissed his bride.

Cal and I entered the reception hall that Wanda and I had transformed the day before. Round tables draped with silver tablecloths dotted the room, and each table held white candles encircled with pink roses. To our right, a buffet table laden with warming dishes invited us to dive in.

We found our seats near the front of the room next to the cake table, which displayed a three-tiered cake adorned with pink and white sugar flowers. Big band music played over the speakers. When Cal and I arrived at our table in the front, Mom and Dan were there with Stella and Dakota.

Cal pulled out my chair, and as I sat, I surveyed the empty seats to my left between Dakota and me. "I wonder who else is going to sit here."

Aunt Rhonda and Uncle Gary had a full table for their family, and Wanda's sons had tables for their families, so they were out.

Hamlet strode over to us.

Cal muttered something under his breath that I couldn't decipher.

Hamlet held out his table card. "It looks like I'm joining you." He shook Dakota's hand, but instead of taking the chair closest to my brother, he hung his suit jacket on the back of the chair next to me and plopped down. "It was so kind of your grandparents to include me since I'm just the sound man."

Cal glared at him.

"Shall we get some appetizers?" Mom asked. "They announced we're free to help ourselves."

"Absolutely." Cal stood up, and we made our way to the table, which held vegetables, dip, crackers, and cheese, as well as assorted fruit.

Even though a rock had taken up residence in my gut, I filled my plate with a couple of crackers, a block of cheese, and three strawberries before winding my way through the tables to our home base.

Hamlet had an extra skip in his step as he returned with a plate stacked with cheese cubes. He swayed along with the music. I hoped he was smart enough not to ask me to dance, or Cal would probably put a fist in his face.

"Hamlet Miller." Mallory approached our table. "Just the man I'm looking for."

This was going to be interesting.

Dakota smirked and put his arm around Stella.

"How may I help you, Mrs. Morris?" Hamlet stood and faced her. "I'm afraid my bachelorette party performance was a one-time deal."

"I know. Too bad. You're quite gifted." She tittered. "Anyway. I've been thinking about what a fine catch you'd be, and I have the perfect young lady in mind for you." She leaned against his chair and tilted her head.

Life Lesson #589: Always travel with a barf bag.

"Really?" He adjusted his tie. "That's very thoughtful. What can you tell me about her?" The dim light did nothing to disguise his red face.

Cal leaned back, crossed his arms, and the edge of his mouth twitched. I didn't dare look at him or I'd erupt into a shriek of laughter for sure. All the tension had to come out somehow.

"Her name is Carmen, and she loves musical theater. She's

my daughter-in-law's sister." Mallory displayed her phone. "Isn't she pretty? She has a nice little figure, too." Mallory winked.

"Actually, Mrs. Morris, that's a picture of a pug."

Hamlet deserved a Tony Award for his straight face and kind tone.

Mallory pressed her hand to her chest. "Oh, silly me. That's my dog, Wiggles. I got this new phone a while back, and I don't know how to use it." She swiped her fingers over the screen. "How about this?" She tipped the phone so he could see.

I strained to get a look. Carmen was dark-haired and gorgeous. I occupied myself with sticking a pepper jack cheese cube on a cracker. It was none of my business anyway.

"Yes, she's attractive," Hamlet said.

Mallory opened her purse, dropped her phone inside, and fished out a piece of paper. "Here's her information."

He reached for the paper but missed and dove for it as Mallory bent over. They collided, and the contents of her purse skittered on the floor as his chair fell backward.

Merciful heavens.

"I'm very sorry. Are you okay?" Hamlet waved the paper in victory before shoving it in his pants pocket and uprighting the chair.

"Of course." Mallory scooped up her purse's contents and shoved them inside. "No harm done. I should've been more careful."

He chuckled. "Don't tell Carmen about this."

She patted him on the shoulder. "I wouldn't dream of it." She tucked her purse under her arm and sauntered away.

Hamlet dropped into his chair. "Well. That was certainly uncomfortable."

We all burst out laughing.

Halfway through dinner, Dakota took his phone from his pocket and glanced at it. A few minutes later, he was still scrolling.

Hamlet nudged me and nodded toward Dakota. "That's why I hate cell phones."

"I know." Dakota often had his face in his phone at family gatherings. It drove me crazy, but I didn't want to irritate my boyfriend by having a side conversation with Hamlet, so I turned my attention to the remaining asparagus spear on my plate.

In spite of the music, Stella must've heard us, because she poked Dakota. "Hello?"

He looked up. "Sorry. I just got a news alert from a story I've been following. The police identified the body the construction workers found a few weeks ago." He turned his phone toward Cal. "Have you helped on the case?"

"Some." His tone made it clear he didn't want to discuss work.

"Who is it?" Hamlet asked.

"Keith Jefferson." Dakota shook his head. "He was from Richardville. I remember hearing about how he disappeared back when Dad was in high school." He turned to Stella. "The poor guy came home from college for the summer, and he went out to run one morning and never came back."

"That's right," Hamlet said. "My mom told me how unsettled all the kids in the area were because they never knew what happened, and there were all kinds of rumors." He glanced at me. "I'm sure his family will be glad to get closure."

I looked at Mom who was busy talking to Dan. "I'm sure." In my lap, I twisted my napkin.

"They found the body in the woods twenty miles from the roads where he usually jogged. What does that mean?" Dakota looked at Cal.

I shoved a piece of chicken around my plate, and Cal shifted. My brother wasn't usually this awkward. Although, maybe I'd never noticed because it ran in the family. Or was this his way of coping with the news about Daddy?

"I can't comment," Cal said. "The investigation is ongoing."

"Ladies and gentlemen, may I have your attention please?" My cousin Eric's voice boomed through the speakers. He'd been asked to be the master of ceremonies since he worked in radio broadcasting. He'd also worn his bacon-print tie for the occasion, much to Aunt Rhonda's dismay. "It's time for the bride and groom to cut the cake."

Grandpa and Wanda walked to the corner where the cake was displayed, and they neatly cut and fed each other a piece, which was no surprise because Grandpa hated watching brides and grooms smash cake in each other's faces.

"Do you think someone hit Keith and then moved his body?" Dakota asked as soon as the cake cutting was over.

The verdict was in. Investigating ran in our family. Nosiness was genetic.

"It's possible." Cal folded his napkin, put it on the table, and stood. "Will you excuse Georgia and me for a moment?"

I was thankful for the escape.

"Babe, put your phone away." Stella gave Dakota a gentle whack on the arm. "Nobody wants to talk about that case right now. We're trying to celebrate."

Trying was the key word.

"Sorry." His cheeks reddened as he stowed his phone in his jacket pocket.

Cal and I walked out of the reception hall, into the foyer, and stood next to the staircase.

"I need to leave." He rested his hands on my upper arms.

"Was it my brother? Because Stella and I can get him to be quiet. He's a lot like me, asking questions when he should keep his mouth shut, and I'm sorry they put Hamlet at our table. I'm sure Wanda did it because he's friends with Dakota, and—"

"It's not your family or Hamlet. It's work. We've had major breaks in two cases, and I can't stay away any longer. I'm sorry about the timing."

"I understand." I tried to hide my disappointment that he wouldn't be there to dance with me.

"Pat's on his way back."

"He doesn't need to—"

"Yes. He does. It'll make me feel better." He met my eyes. "Are you okay?"

"Yes." I said the word with more conviction than I felt.

"I'll call you later." He kissed me on the cheek and strode out the door.

I took a few deep breaths before I turned and trudged toward the reception hall.

"Now, I need all the single ladies to join the bride on the dance floor," Eric said. "Georgia, that means you too."

I froze in the doorway and flashed my dear cousin a tight smile.

Life Lesson #6008: Never trust a man wearing a bacon-print tie.

As usual, my timing was impeccable, and since this wasn't a huge wedding, there weren't exactly many single ladies.

"Come on out, Georgia."

I plodded to the middle of the dance floor but waved at the crowd. A couple of Wanda's widowed friends joined me, along with Fiona Sylvan and two preteen girls who stood next to each other giggling and ducking their heads.

Fantastic. Not only was this situation embarrassing, but I had too many other things on my mind. Beverly's murder. Daddy's murder. Clara's murder. Cal's current case overload. All the secrets past—and present.

"Go, Georgia!" Dakota wolf-whistled. Apparently, he'd been taking notes from Preston and Austin on how to be annoying.

Wanda turned her back to her bouquet-toss victims, and I vowed to be a good sport for Grandpa's sake.

"On my count," Eric said. "One. Two. Three."

Wanda hurled the flowers over her head. The two older ladies raised their hands. Fiona stepped back. The girls rushed forward, while I made a half-hearted attempt to lift my arms.

The bouquet ricocheted off the disco ball and plummeted toward the girls. Good. They could fight over it.

One girl batted at the other but whacked the flowers instead. This sent them hurtling toward my face.

I swiped at the bridal projectile, my finger snagging a loop of silver ribbon.

A ribbon just like Clara's.

From prom night.

In May 1980.

The crowd cheered, and I raised the unwanted flowers in forced victory, because I was almost sure that one night held the answer to three unsolved murders.

CHAPTER TWENTY-THREE

I had to ask Fiona another question—just to make sure my theory was right. Maybe it was wishful thinking, and after all the recent stress and years of waiting for answers about Daddy, I'd concocted a ridiculous solution.

I clutched the bouquet and turned toward her. "Fio—"

"I need a picture with you and the bride." The scrawny photographer blocked my path. He pointed to Wanda, who was beaming.

"Sure." I tried to keep the panic from my voice as Fiona walked back to her table and laughed with the other museum volunteers. I put my arm around Wanda's waist and gripped the bouquet.

"Awww! That'll make a nice picture. Big smiles." He raised the camera.

I managed to comply.

"She'll be next," Wanda said to the photographer as I escaped the dance floor and wove my way to Fiona's table.

"All right, single gentlemen, it's your turn. Come on out for the garter toss," Eric said.

Michelle rushed over and grabbed the microphone out of his hand. "You too, little brother."

Good work, Michelle.

"Fiona." I scurried over to her seat.

"Nice catch." She picked up her water goblet.

I knelt next to her. "Thanks. One follow-up question from something we were talking about earlier today."

She took a drink. "Sure."

"You said Mallory wrapped her car around a tree back in high school, right?"

She furrowed her brow, which was quite a feat considering her love of Botox. "Yes."

"When?" I clutched the bouquet.

"Prom night. Well—it was probably the morning after a night of partying. She was so drunk she missed the driveway and hit that big maple in her dad's front yard." Fiona sniffed. "You know, the weird thing was, after Clara and I started talking again years later, she told me they hit a deer that night." Fiona shrugged. "I guess she was so drunk she thought a tree was a deer."

Try Keith Jefferson.

I scanned the room. Mallory was nowhere to be found. "Thanks, Fiona."

Eric and Hamlet, along with a few young boys, stood in the middle of the dance floor as I darted back to the table, tossed the bouquet aside, and snatched my purse. "I need to make a phone call. I'll be right back."

No one responded because my family was engrossed in watching Grandpa trying to remove Wanda's garter as discreetly and quickly as possible. Frankly, I was stunned he'd even agreed to the spectacle.

I kept an eye on the action as I high-tailed it toward the foyer. Grandpa slid the garter off Wanda's leg and tossed it over his shoulder in one motion. The low pitch seemed destined for one of the little boys, but at the last second, Hamlet reached his long arm out and intercepted it.

The crowd cheered as I burst into the hallway and made my way to the foyer. Two women lingered next to the restroom door, deep in conversation, but the vast room caused the voices to echo, and I could hear their conversation about taking meals to one of their sick friends.

Wanting privacy, I pushed my way outside and yanked my phone from my purse. The weather had turned cold again, and the wind blowing across the barren fields punched through my lacy sleeves as I tapped Cal's number.

"Pick up, Cal." I paced beside the tractor in front of the reception hall. His voice mail kicked on. I closed my eyes. "It's me. I figured out who killed Keith Jefferson and how his death is relat—"

A strong arm clamped around my throat, and a hand pressed against my mouth. I kicked and tried to scream as someone dragged me around the corner.

Earl, in a baseball cap and flannel jacket, appeared beside me, yanked my phone away, and disconnected. "Sorry to crash your celebration, Miss Georgia."

"But we can't let you talk," Mallory whispered and tightened her grip on my neck, and I struggled for a breath.

Earl's fingers tapped against my phone's screen as he walked toward a dumpster. Mallory followed, dragging me along. Hamlet's silver sedan idled behind the dumpster.

My limbs weakened. Surely Hamlet wasn't . . . ?

My phone buzzed, and Earl glanced at it. "Hamlet's on his way." He wiped off the phone and tossed it into the dumpster before leaning into the car and popping the trunk.

If I could get away from Mallory, I could definitely outrun Earl.

"You should've minded your own business." Without loosening her grip, Mallory shoved me toward the trunk.

When I flailed, Earl slapped my face. I winced and lost my balance on my high heels. Earl and Mallory overpowered me and shoved me into the trunk. I screamed as she slammed the lid.

Darkness enclosed me.

"Mrs. Morris?" Hamlet's deep voice cut into my coffin. "Where's Georgia? She texted Dakota and told him to tell me to come out. What's going—?"

Thwack.

A muffled moan. "Geor—"

"Hamlet!" I yelled.

Thwack!

"Help!" Panic rose in my chest as I realized Mallory and Earl's plan. They were going to kill me and frame Hamlet. Mallory's fix-up ruse had been to steal Hamlet's keys.

I pounded against the trunk and screamed. "Help!"

"Give me the ribbon," Mallory barked.

Was she really tying up Hamlet with decorative ribbon?

A door slammed. Then another. And another. The engine revved.

I searched for the emergency trunk release, but there was no glow-in-the-dark handle hanging down like in Brandi's Fusion. When she'd purchased the car, we'd joked about how good it would be to have that if you were ever trapped. Either this car didn't have an emergency release, or Earl or Mallory had been smart enough to clip it.

"Hamlet? Are you okay?" I yelled and pounded the panel between the trunk and the back seat.

The muffled hum of the engine and tires against the road answered.

God, please help us.

What were my other options? I ran my fingers around the

edge of the trunk floor, searching for the hollow that contained the spare tire. Was there a tire iron I could use to pry open the trunk?

Rolling aside, I tugged the floor upward and thrust my hand down, feeling for a tire. Instead, I found an empty well.

No spare? Seriously?

Time for Plan B.

Drawing my knees to my chest, I reached for my shoes with the three-inch heels and slipped them off. I placed them next to my chest, so I'd be ready if I couldn't punch out a taillight and get someone's attention before we stopped.

Shifting to my side, I searched for brake light wires but encountered a solid panel instead. *Please, God, help someone find us.* I dug my nails along the panel and gave it a tug, but it held fast. As the car turned the corner, I braced myself.

I rolled over on my other side and examined the trunk's back wall for pass-through access to the backseat. My fingers rested on the opening, and I tugged it.

Nothing. It needed to release from the other side.

Gravel crackled under tires.

The car stopped.

No!

Rolling onto my back, I gripped a shoe in each hand with the heels facing out. A door slammed.

"You sure about this, sweetheart?" Earl asked.

"Dad, it's perfect," Mallory said. "Hamlet told anyone who'd listen about how he's fixing this house a little at a time. His next project is filling the old pool. We'll use this gun and leave it behind to make it look like Georgia figured out that Hamlet was the one who vandalized the grain elevator years ago and killed her dad. We'll stage the scene to appear that Hamlet planned to bury Georgia here but was overcome with remorse and killed himself."

"How you gonna explain Hamlet killing Bev? That ain't gonna make sense to folks."

"I can make it look like Beverly suspected Hamlet killed Ray, and when Hamlet found out, he broke in and killed her. Now that Clara's dead, there's no eyewitness to the shooting."

"How you gonna do that?"

"Technology," Mallory said. "Don't worry about it. I stole back the phone Beverly bought from me, and it's still connected to my cloud storage account."

That was why Mallory had killed Beverly. She'd heard the voice notes Beverly took at the museum and knew she was getting suspicious.

Dread swelled my throat, threatening to choke off my oxygen. The only thing I could think to do was stall. I thumped my fist against the top of the trunk. "Hey, masterminds. Before you finish us off, we'd like some answers."

Seconds ticked by, and my pulse thudded against my neck. Why had I gone the smart-aleck route? I curled my fingers around my shoes and readied myself to strike.

"We're going to pop the trunk," Mallory said. "And the first thing you're going to see is a gun, so I strongly advise you not to try anything."

My heart constricted, and I released my grip on my high-heeled weapons.

The trunk opened, and I sat up and raised my shaking hands in surrender. Mallory and Earl stood on either side of the car with guns aimed at me.

They'd driven behind Hamlet's house and parked next to the gaping hole that'd once been the pool. A pile of jagged concrete pieces rested near the trees that swayed in the bitter wind.

I shivered.

My stomach twisted. Nine and a half years. My family had

waited all that time while my neighbor and his daughter held the answers about Daddy's murder.

"Don't move. Tell me what you know—and who you've told." Mallory narrowed her eyes.

"You got three seconds to start talking." Earl waved his gun.

"Okay, okay! I haven't told anyone—anything." I closed my eyes and tried to sort the pieces falling into place. "Detective Perkins told us tonight that the same weapon used in Beverly's murder was also used in Daddy's murder." I opened my eyes.

Mallory and Earl exchanged glances.

"Duh." Her pretty features twisted, and for the first time, she looked haggard. "I overheard. Why do you think we're here? What else do you know?"

My mind swirled. "You both have a long history of covering up murders. It's quite the family heritage." I shuddered and stared at Mallory. "It all began back in high school when you and Clara Alspaugh were hanging out. You were popular. You had a basketball scholarship for college. After prom, you and Clara went to a party and had too much to drink. Maybe did some drugs. Early the next morning, you were driving home. That's when you hit Keith Jefferson and killed him."

She didn't flinch. "Go on."

"Clara had passed out, but the accident roused her enough that she asked questions. You told her you hit a deer and took her home. If you reported the wreck, you'd jeopardize your college scholarship. Earl didn't want that to happen either." I fixed my gaze on him. "I'm guessing you helped Mallory move Keith's body twenty miles away from the scene of her accident."

"I took care of it myself." He lifted his chin. "My little girl didn't have no business burying a body."

How sweet. I nodded at Mallory. "Then, you drove your car into a tree in your front yard to hide the front-end damage."

"Well aren't you smart," she said.

I looked at Earl. "Did your wife know?"

"Nope. She'd gone to visit her sister in Kentucky. This was between Mallory and me."

My leg tingled thanks to my awkward position in the trunk. "You were afraid Clara would remember what happened, so you started rumors about her to drive her out of town."

Mallory smirked. "Clara was always gullible."

"Meanwhile, you went to college and lived your life like nothing happened."

"And I'm not going to let you ruin everything I've worked for." She tightened her grip on her revolver.

I squinted at Earl as I pieced together my daddy's role. "Everything was fine until Daddy served on the football reunion committee with you, right?"

"All them recollections about high school must've jogged something in Ray's memory." His expression hardened. "I went in to work at the museum one day and caught him nosing around in the microfiche files, looking for articles about Keith Jefferson's disappearance. Ray played it off nice and smooth, but I knew something was up."

"Plus, you overheard Daddy ask Fiona Sylvan for Clara's address, so then you panicked. You knew about the vandalism at Bill Alspaugh's grain elevator and figured Daddy would drive by after the school board meeting and stop if he saw something wrong." My throat thickened. "And when he did, you shot him and staged the scene to look like he'd interrupted a robbery."

"I had to protect my daughter." His hand trembled, but he kept his grip on the gun.

Rustling sounded in the car. What was Hamlet doing back there?

I looked at Mallory. "Did you have any idea before tonight that Earl killed my daddy?"

"No." The muscle in her jaw twitched. "I didn't suspect, or I never would've borrowed his gun."

"I had no reason to tell her about Ray," Earl said. "Never thought she'd go and kill people on purpose. I was mighty shocked when she called and asked for my help tonight."

They glared at each other. I had to keep distracting them before they took out their anger on Hamlet and me.

"As long as Clara stayed in Texas, you felt like your secret was safe." I focused on Mallory and raised my voice to cover the vibrations from Hamlet's movements.

"When Clara decided to come home after those construction workers found Keith's body, I was afraid she'd remember we hadn't hit a deer that night. Plus, her nosy mother was still curious about the Keith Jefferson case because I heard her voice notes in my cloud storage account. Then Beverly taunted me by giving me those old prom pictures." Mallory scowled. "I had to do something before she and Clara started talking."

Earl's eyes flashed. "You shoulda left well enough alone."

Click. Swoosh.

I felt certain Hamlet had managed to crack open the pass through from the back seat, but I had no way to confirm my suspicions without turning around. But why would he risk upsetting them?

Then it hit me.

Hamlet carried his phone. In his car.

Could he have dialed 9-1-1 with his tied hands?

Please, God. Let it be true.

Either way, I *had* to keep Earl and Mallory talking. "Earl has an alibi for the barn fire, so it had to be you." I shifted my numb leg and turned to Mallory. "I never would've taken you for a pyromaniac."

"I don't suppose you would've taken me for a shooter either." Her face remained expressionless.

197

"True. You overheard Wanda on the phone with me asking about the trees and decided to go for a two-for-one deal and get rid of Clara and me."

"Enough!" Mallory shouted. "Dad, get Hamlet out of the car."

Swoosh. Click.

She kept her weapon pointed at me as Earl opened the door to the backseat. I held my breath, hoping Hamlet would manage to hide his phone—if he'd been able to get to it.

"Slide out nice and slow." Earl kept his gun aimed at Hamlet.

With his hands bound behind his back, Hamlet emerged from the car and met my gaze. "Are you hurt?"

"N-not yet." I did a lousy job of keeping the tremor out of my voice. Then I fought a badly timed burst of stress laughter. They *had* used silver ribbon to tie Hamlet's hands.

Earl slammed the door shut. A look of calm determination settled over Hamlet's features when Earl pressed the gun into his side.

"You." Mallory waved her gun at me. "Get out of the trunk."

I climbed out, and my panty-hose clad feet protested as the rocks bit into them. My sleeping leg buckled. Goosebumps covered my entire body, and stray snowflakes swirled around us.

"Move toward the pool," Mallory said.

"You mean the gaping hole in the ground that used to be the *Williams family's pool?*" I shouted before clenching my jaw to keep my teeth from chattering.

"Shut up and march." Hate flared in Mallory's eyes.

I took a measured step into the dead grass. The faint sound of an approaching vehicle hummed.

"Faster!" Mallory shouted.

I took another step forward, and my heart sank when the vehicle sped by the house.

Please, God.

"I'd like to say something to Georgia before you kill us," Hamlet said.

I stopped about ten feet away from the hole and turned around with my hands up.

Mallory rolled her eyes. "Seriously?"

"Let him talk," Earl said. "It's plain as day the guy has feelings for her."

"He's stalling." Mallory pressed her lips together.

"I wanna hear it," Earl said. "Don't you remember what it was like to be young and in love?"

"Fine." Mallory glared at Earl and then flicked her gaze to Hamlet. "Thirty seconds."

"When I moved back to Wildcat Springs, I wanted to be close to my family to start my new business. But I'm going to be honest now that we're facing death. I had you in the back of my mind, Georgia Rae Winston."

I closed my eyes.

"I've been wanting to date you for years, but before now I was always too young."

Not all that long ago, I'd asked myself how much trauma one person could take. At the time, I didn't know what trauma was. That was minor drama compared to everything that had happened to me during the last few months.

"I don't know what to say." I didn't have the strength to start babbling.

"Then just listen. I didn't admit it to myself until you walked into Latte Conspiracies, but I saw you and didn't want to let you go without a fight. I knew you were taken, so I should've known my place."

"It's okay," I whispered.

"No. It's not. I apologize. You belong with Detective Perkins. He makes you happy, and I have no desire to interfere. After I sell this house, I'm leaving town and settling elsewhere."

"Hamlet, you don't have to—"

Mallory snickered. "What're you talking about? Neither one of you are settling anywhere." She waved her gun at Hamlet and then pointed to where I was standing. "Get over here."

He walked over and stood beside me. "Three, two, one . . ." he whispered.

"Richard County Sheriff's Department! Lower your weapons!"

CHAPTER TWENTY-FOUR

Hamlet and I sat in the back seat of Cal's car with the heat blasting and waited to give our official statements. A kind deputy had found blankets for us.

Mallory and Earl had already been led away from the scene in handcuffs. Hamlet had quite the bump on his head from where Earl had clocked him, but other than being a little frozen, we'd both be fine.

"Did you mean everything you said, or were you stalling?" I asked.

"Yes."

"Hamlet . . ."

He looked out the window. "I saw Detective Perkins and the deputies rushing around the perimeter, so I bought them some time."

"I see." I wrapped the blanket around my shoulders.

"He's a good man."

"I know."

The silence took a left turn into awkward territory. "How'd you manage to dial 9-1-1 with your hands tied up?"

He chuckled. "My phone fell under the seat on the way to the wedding, and it slid out while they were driving. When they left the car, I picked it up and dialed with my nose."

"Your nose?" I blinked at him. "That takes talent."

"Thank you." He tapped his nose and grinned.

"No. Thank *you* for saving our lives."

"It was a joint effort thanks to your well-honed detective skills." He patted my shoulder, and I pushed away the pinch of regret that he'd be leaving town. It shouldn't matter.

Should it?

Mom gathered me in a hug as soon as I walked through the back door of my house with Cal at my heels. Though it was almost midnight, a fresh pot of coffee waited on the counter, and Gus scurried over to greet us. I scratched his head.

Dan sat at my kitchen table with Dakota, Stella, Aunt Rhonda, and Uncle Gary. One by one, they each got up and gave me a hug.

Dan shook Cal's hand. "Good work, Detective."

"Thanks." His lips flattened, and he surveyed my family.

Mom poured coffee into my owl mug, stirred in some cream, set it on the table, and motioned to the empty chair. "Sit, sweetie. It's decaf, so you can sleep."

"I had decaf?" Normally, I considered the stuff a waste of time.

"No, but we stopped at the convenience store, and Dan bought some for you because I figured you wouldn't have any." She turned and poured a cup for Cal who stood next to the counter.

I took a sip and looked at my stepdad. "Thanks."

He smiled ruefully.

"I can't believe it's finally over," Dakota said. "We know who killed Dad."

Stella put her arm around Dakota.

I set my mug on the table. "Who's going to tell Grandpa?"

"I'll do it," Aunt Rhonda said. "Tomorrow morning before he and Wanda leave on their honeymoon." She met my gaze. "If it's okay with all of you."

"Absolutely," Dakota said.

"That's fine with me," Mom said.

"Yes." As much as I loved Grandpa, I didn't have the strength to break the news. "Thank you."

Aunt Rhonda nodded, and Uncle Gary took her hand.

It was going to take a while to process everything that'd happened.

The next day, after sleeping until noon, I woke up a with a mission in mind. After making myself look presentable—a difficult task thanks to some massive bags under my eyes—I drove to a grocery store in Richardville and purchased a dozen yellow roses. I chose that color because it contrasted with the drabness of the late winter afternoon.

Then I made my way to the Wildcat Springs Cemetery and followed the winding drive up to the graves. It didn't take me long to find Beverly's—piled with wilting flowers from her funeral. I parked, got out, and cleared away the dead flowers. After dumping them in the back of my truck, I took half of my new roses and placed them on the fresh mound of dirt.

"We found the murderers, Beverly." I sniffed. "I know you can't hear me because you're having a ball up in heaven with

Jesus and your friends and family." I shoved my hands into my coat pockets. "But I just needed to thank you for your friendship —and for your prayers that we'd find Daddy's killer." I buried my face in my hands. "I just wish you hadn't been part of the answer."

Taking a shuddering breath, I returned to my truck and drove down the gravel path to the opposite end of the graveyard where Daddy was buried. Every spring, Mom had been faithful to put artificial flowers in the vases on either side of the stone, but she removed them every fall, so they stood empty.

I'd only been able to bring myself to visit once, about six months after Daddy had died. With the rest of the roses in hand, I made my way toward his headstone and placed the flowers in each of the vases.

"You finally have justice," I whispered and ran my hand over the smooth granite, then sat in the brown grass and wished for the millionth time that he were here to advise me.

The next Sunday afternoon, I played hymns on the piano while Gus snoozed on his bed near the fireplace.

Cal would be here any minute.

It had been a rough week thanks to interviews with the media, Clara's funeral, and uncertainty about my relationship with Cal. After praying for answers, I'd finally asked Cal over to talk. Before today, his busyness at work had offered me the perfect excuse for stalling.

Stay strong, Georgia Rae.

A knock sounded on my back door, and I placed the furniture polish and rag in my utility room before hustling to answer. "Hey, Cal. Come on in." I stepped aside. "Have a seat." I pointed to the kitchen table.

He gazed at me with an expression I couldn't quite read, but he sat, and Gus entered to see what was happening. Cal scratched his head. "Hey, boy."

Gus panted and sniffed Cal's leg.

"How's Miss Peacock?" I asked.

"Fine. Denise told me I could keep her since she already has a dog of her own, and she has enough going on, trying to work things out with Jack." He shook his head. "I can't believe I'm going to have a dog named *Miss Peacock*."

I smiled.

"How does it feel to have your dad's case solved?" he asked.

I sat across from him. "Wonderful. But painful to know my neighbor did it."

"Yeah. I can imagine." He studied me. "But you didn't ask me here to talk about the case."

"No." I folded my hands and rested them on the table. My pulse thrummed in my neck, and I forced my brain to get on topic instead of running wild into other possible subjects on which I could babble for a good ten minutes.

Spit it out.

"Where's our relationship going?" I asked.

Cal was silent for what had to be a full ten seconds, which ticked by at injured tortoise speed. "What do you mean?" He furrowed his brow. "We've only been dating a few months."

I blew out a breath. Not what I'd been hoping for, though his response was what I'd expected. "Right. But we're not teenagers, and a few months is enough to know if we're heading for marriage or for burnout. I'm not asking you to propose right this minute. But I'm wondering if that's a possibility in the future."

"It's too soon for me to know for sure." He shifted.

"That's why you bought a house."

He crossed his arms. "It was exactly what I was looking for."

"It didn't take long to decide on that, did it?"

He scowled. "Marriage isn't the same as buying a house, Georgia."

I flipped my braid back and forth between my fingers. "It's not just about the house. You don't whistle any more. When I met you, and we first started dating, you whistled all the time."

"I've been through the wringer the last three weeks." He let out a cynical laugh. "You're basing the health of our relationship on the fact that I'm not whistling?"

I understood he'd been overwhelmed, but if a man were in love, wouldn't he whistle *more*? Wouldn't the world, even with all the death and darkness in it, seem like a happier place because of finding the person you wanted to spend your life with?

"Yes." I met his eyes. "I'm also basing my assessment on your refusal to attend my Bible study."

"We've talked about that. It's not my thing."

"Studying the Bible with my friends isn't your thing?"

"It's something I do every week at church and on my own, so I'm good."

"Look, I'm willing to give up my church and go to yours if our relationship progresses, but I won't abandon my friends. Your unwillingness to get to know them freaks me out. They're taking it personally, and so am I."

He shook his head. "I don't get it. We have a good thing going. Why are you trying to ruin it by bringing all this stuff up?"

I squeezed my hands together. "I'm trying to avoid moving forward and causing a bigger mess in the future because we didn't solve our problems when they were small." I spoke with more resolve than I felt.

"This is about Hamlet, isn't it? I heard him say he wants to date you." He gazed at me with such intensity that I had sympathy for suspects he interrogated.

"No. Didn't you hear the part about Hamlet leaving town?

The problem isn't him. It's you holding back. I know you care about me, but you're not all in, and I don't know why."

"I'm sorry." He crossed his arms. "It's complicated."

"How?"

"I'm just going through some things right now that you don't know about."

"What things? Your parents' divorce?"

"Partly."

"Is it another woman? An old girlfriend?"

"No."

"What else is there?" What was he hiding?

"I don't want to talk about it."

I bristled. "Why not?"

"Because I don't. My life isn't a mystery you need to solve." His eyes flashed.

My breath caught as I froze. "Is that why you're holding back? Because you resent that I've helped solve your cases?" Tears pricked my eyes.

"No. As much as I wish you wouldn't put yourself in danger, that's not it." He refused to meet my gaze. "You've been a valuable asset."

Romantic words every woman dreamed of hearing.

I pressed my fingers against my eyebrows. How could our relationship progress if he wouldn't share what was bothering him? If he didn't trust me with his concerns? I looked up. "Do you love me?" I blurted the words before I could think through the consequences.

Cal stared at his hands. "I care about you. A lot."

"I know. But do you *love* me?"

He lifted his head. "I don't know."

But I did. "Then we need to break up, because clearly, this relationship isn't right."

"You broke up with Cal, didn't you?" Brandi asked as she and Ashley stood in my foyer later that night.

"I don't show for Bible study, and that's your conclusion?" Though my puffy eyes and red nose were probably pretty huge clues. I clutched a crumpled tissue. "And people call *me* the detective. Good guess, girls." I managed a shaky laugh.

They each hugged me.

"Come on in," I said.

None of us said a word as we filed into my living room and took our usual spots on my sectional sofa. Why did we always sit in the same places?

"What happened?" Ashley asked.

I gave them a brief summary of Cal's refusal to share what was going on in his life. "Plus, he doesn't whistle anymore." I stuffed my hands in the front pocket of my Colts hoodie. "I know that sounds crazy, but—"

"It doesn't," Ashley said.

"Not at all," Brandi whispered.

"You've sensed something's been off for a while, haven't you?" I asked.

Brandi nodded, her curls bouncing. "I've been praying that God's will would be done, but I was always cheering for your relationship. I know how much you like Cal."

"Same here, hon."

"Breaking up was the right choice. I feel at peace for the first time in several weeks."

Why had I ignored my uncertainty? Probably because I wanted my own way instead of what God wanted. Pretty typical human response.

Brandi scooted closer. "I'd hate to give you false hope, but just because you've ended things with Cal doesn't mean God's done with this story. It could be the timing is wrong, and things have to get worse before they get better."

I nodded. *A time to tear down, and a time to rebuild.*

Part of me hoped this was the case, and that Cal could resolve whatever was troubling him and be able to move forward.

"Right," Ashley said. "God might have stuff he wants to do in your lives individually."

"Or I'm supposed to be single forever." I sniffed. I'd been see-sawing between optimism and pessimism all evening.

Brandi smiled. "Maybe. But I don't think either one of us was going to add that possibility right at this moment."

Ashley shook her head. "No way."

"I appreciate that."

"You'll be fine." Ashley put her arm around me. "You've got us."

"Absolutely," Brandi said.

Though my heart ached, I felt hopeful about my future. I had my friends. Family. My health. My canine sidekick, Gus. A job I loved. Music.

And a God who'd already proven himself faithful during difficult times.

Yeah—I'd be way better than fine.

Don't miss Georgia's next adventure in *Deadly Harmony*! Stay in touch by subscribing to my email newsletter at www.marissashrock.com. You'll get the latest on all my new releases and other fun updates.

As a thank you for subscribing, you'll gain access to *Deadly Homestead: A Georgia Rae Winston Mini-Mystery and Other Short Stories.*

If you enjoyed *Deadly Heritage*, I'd be very grateful if you'd leave a short review to help me spread the word about my novels.

ABOUT THE AUTHOR

Jenni Mansell Photography

Marissa Shrock is a survivor of many awkward blind dates and many years of teaching middle school. Both provide excellent inspiration for her fictional yarns.

Since childhood, she's loved to read a variety of genres, so her own work includes dystopian thrillers and cozy mysteries. She's the author of the Emancipation Warriors Series and the Georgia Rae Winston Mystery Series. Her debut novel, *The First Principle*, was a Carol Award Finalist.

Marissa enjoys playing golf, building elaborate LEGO creations, and traveling to new places. Her home is in Indiana, where she's surrounded by corn and soybean fields. Visit her at www.marissashrock.com.

ALSO BY MARISSA SHROCK

ACKNOWLEDGMENTS

Editing by A Little Red Ink

Cover Art by Seedlings Design Studio

Marketing Copy by JR2 Marketing & Advertising

Cimelia Press Logo by Race Point

Beta Readers: Mary Shrock, Brad Shrock, Katie Briggs, and Julie Woodall

www.ingramcontent.com/pod-product-compliance
Lightning Source LLC
Chambersburg PA
CBHW061146170626
46809CB00003B/999